PENGUIN BOO
KAIKA'S SON

M.A. MODHAYAN is a devoted father and husband. A middle child, yet an elder brother. A debut writer, with deep interest in music history and theory. Mostly inspired by man-made gods, the concept of time, futurism, and humanism. *Kaika's Songs* is his debut novel.

KaiKa's Songs

by
M.A. Modhayan

PENGUIN BOOKS
An imprint of Penguin Random House

PENGUIN BOOKS

USA | Canada | UK | Ireland | Australia
New Zealand | India | South Africa | China

Penguin Books is part of the Penguin Random House group of companies
whose addresses can be found at global.penguinrandomhouse.com

Published by Penguin Random House India Pvt. Ltd
4th Floor, Capital Tower 1, MG Road,
Gurugram 122 002, Haryana, India

First published in Penguin Books by Penguin Random House India 2022

All rights reserved

10 9 8 7 6 5 4 3 2 1

ISBN 9780143459125

Typeset in Sabon LT Std by Digiultrabooks Pvt. Ltd

www.penguin.co.in

To May, Khalifa, Theia, and Rheia

This is a story about the survival of
men, women, gods, and songs.

Contents

Prologue

Everything
revolves around Sand
over here on Sand Island.
Who eats, and who starves.
Who leads, and who serves.
Who sees, and who's blind.
Who's born, and who dies.
Everything happens
by Sand's
command.
Sand is in charge of Sand Island.
Time stops with the arrival of Sand,
and time moves again
when Sand
disbands

xii   Prologue

Sand is blinding; no one can gaze into Sand's eyes. Sand is suffocating; no one can seize a breath while it flies. Sand is fatally painful. It scrapes the skin off, revealing nerves and bloody muscle tissues. Sand is painfully fatal. It burns the body in its darkest shadows. Sand is mischievously wicked. It makes the wise lose their minds. Sand is maliciously playful. It makes death something to wish for. Something the brave would not mind.

No armour is strong enough to withstand Sand monsters. No one can ever win a battle against Sand.

When Sand monsters come and trap the living inside their caves, the living live a fleeting life immersed in the darkest shadow of all shadows: in thirst, hunger, madness, terror, suspicion, aggression, and no glimpse of hope at all.

Astray snakes and lizards, thirsty mice, and lost birds crawl through the cavern's cracks and holes, terrified of Sand and welcomed by the starving band.

With every sandstorm and tornado, islanders lose a chief or a thief, or an innocent child or two. Death inside the caves comes to those who were lucky to age and those who are ill. Death comes to those who are carried by their mothers, unborn still. And occasionally, or rather seasonally, death comes when men kill. And with each life lost, gloomy feasts follow that are barely fulfilling for those left alive.

When Sand calms down and flies away, the sky bleeds for less than a quarter of a day. But when the walls of the cave are acutely dry and an islander is about to die, even a tiny drop is easy to sense. Just a touch of moisture can end the suspense. That is how they know it is safe to leave and release their children into the open. It is finally safe to dig themselves out of their prison.

Each time a sandstorm retreats and a tornado ceases, islanders find their world completely changed; nothing is the way it used to be. Sand always wipes away their footprints. Sand shuffles the features of their island's face. New terrain, new dunes, new burrows, new little ponds, new rocks to play with, new leaders to obey and follow, newly born islanders to nurture, and new collections of bones and skulls to lend and borrow.

After spending timeless nights in the darkness of their caves, the islanders now willingly spend more time under the shade of the cave. They avoid the light before they run into the open, for some have lost their sight by looking straight into the eye of the sun after spending long nights in prison. The moon's light is gentler for them to navigate their world. Starvation casts its shadow on islanders even after the departure of Sand. Yet, the clear air they breathe, the soft light of the moon, and the tranquil breeze they feel are satisfying enough for their bodies and minds to not ask for more.

Every day and night, the islanders keep singing all their songs to Sand.

To sing, and to keep singing, is what Sand commands.

After all, Sand is in charge of Sand Island. And as long as Sand is in charge, the islanders must never stop singing.

Everything revolves around Sand, here, on Sand Island.

Part I
Sand Island

Chapter One
Songs of Hunger and Thirst

Several sandstorms have passed since KaiKa's mother died.

The last mother on Sand Island left behind the last five children, the last islanders. Two short young women, two tall young men, and a little blind girl.

KaiKa was the leader of her tiny tribe. There were NooaKhi and LaKhi, the last two men on Sand Island. They were both KaiKa's half-brothers. Then there was SeeKa, KaiKa's half-sister. And all four of them provided food, water, and protection for AiYi, the little half-bald blind girl who always followed KaiKa wherever she went, like a loving domesticated pet. She was no one's sister.

All five young islanders walked around in the wilderness of Sand Island, naked but always covered with dirt and flies. Islanders had made peace with the flies that covered their bodies since the day they were granted their first dose of consciousness. Those flies traveled with them wherever they went, as if they were extended useless limbs for some islanders and common accessories for others.

They were all dark-skinned, gaunt, dirty, and had rough, dry palms. They had long, untamed hair, and unapologetically ungroomed pubic and armpit hair. They all had beards. The men had long beards with few hairless patches on their cheeks and heads. They all produced nauseating odours that they barely noticed. Blind little AiYi, on the other hand, used each islander's scent and voice, like facial features to give each islander an identity. That is how she recognized them.

Scars, blotches, and blisters marked the islanders' bodies and faces like the marks on a piece of sedimentary rock. Hair covered their bodies and faces. Like hooves of the mighty elephant, the islanders' feet and heels were cracked and thick enough to walk on hot, rough rocks without feeling any pain or discomfort. Like the knees of the dark brown desert camel, the islanders' knees and elbows were covered with thick, knobbly grey dead skin. Every knee was as distinguished as their faces. Like the wild goat's horns, their fingernails and toenails were long, hardened, and darkened by dirt reservoirs. Some were broken, and some had spiralled.

While their bodies were infested with famine and death, their eyes were like oases, rich with life. Their smiles were genuinely unthreatening and despondent. All but AiYi had missing molars and incisors and dark receding gums. Teeth that were not missing were black or yellow and either erupted or broken. Yet, they were the most gorgeous living beings one could find on Sand Island.

Two enormous granite rock mountain beds stood high at the heart of Sand Island. The first bed was confused between reds and browns, and the other was a certain shade of grey. One could look at the island from a mountain top and swear that the red-brown mountain bed fell from the sky and landed over the massive dark grey rock. The two rock mountains had cracked, shattered, and scattered around Sand Island. The rocks were covered and surrounded by white dunes filled with ancient seashells and sparkles of bleached corals that looked like the remains of ground skulls.

A few rocks had slid into the sea and were wrapped by paths of jagged white sea salt formations and coral ruins. One rock looked like a giant primordial shark that had died swallowing a giant sea lion and left nothing but its giant jaws intact. The sea lion trapped between the shark's teeth with its flattened tail dipped into the sea forever.

Shade was not to be found other than under small clouds that must have lost their way over the island or inside the crusty old caves, narrow cracks and passages, and under giant rocks that had settled over other giant old rocks.

Depending on the dunes' continuously changing patterns, traveling from the west coast to the island's eastern edge could take an audacious half-day of walking. And traveling from the northern tip of the island to its southern coast could take an entire day of recklessness. While the inner terrains of the island were easier to navigate, walking around the island at midday and gazing outwards into the ocean's horizon was as useless as looking into a broken compass. The island was childless; there were no grey silhouettes of other islands as far as the eye could see. The sea was deep right under the islanders' noses. Even if islanders knew how to swim, there was nothing to swim to. And the lowest tides always failed to uncover any juvenile sand or coral islands. Sand Island was utterly isolated from any other incubators of any form of existence.

The ocean was even grumpier and stingier than the land itself. It was like a merciless despicable warden that held the island and its inhabitants in captivity for its own amusement. Its water was acutely salty, and its waves were loud and violent, with a strong appetite to eat any living being Sand could toss into its plate. The ocean used the wave like a whip that was often and regularly used to lash and warn the islanders from getting close to its waters.

While serving inmates with regular meals was common among the most merciless wardens, the ocean did not care to carry any edible beasts or plants into the island's empty dry trays. And no islander had ever successfully left the shores without being eaten by the sea and pulled away into its stomach. So, the islanders never dared to touch seawater that was in direct contact with the ocean. However, they had learnt that the shore's seawater had healing qualities, especially in ponds of sea salt rock formations. They only made contact with water that had lost its way into a pond far from the tides, detached from its parent, the ocean.

Although food and life were far from being abundant on Sand Island, it was home to a handful of small animals, insects, and plants scarcely scattered across the island. Water was equally scarce too. Islanders could find freshwater either in tiny murky ponds of rainwater from the brief showers that happened after sandstorms, or in small tenebrous ponds hidden inside the dark caverns.

The five islanders had no cattle to herd, no crops to farm, no wicker to weave, no shelters to build or maintain, and no grains to sift and grind. So, they kept themselves alive by doing as little as possible and spent most of their time napping and resting inside the caves; laying down, stretching, and yawning all day long. They often saved their energy to perform quick daytime cacti fruit-gathering labour tasks and nocturnal mouse hunting.

A fire had no chance of survival on an island filled with sand, seawater, and monstrous sandstorms and tornadoes. Sand Island was a suffocating environment for fire. With the absence of wood and dried leaves, coupled with the abundance of sand, the island was not a hospitable place for a flare to breathe. They were deprived of the gifts of fire. They never experienced the warmth fire could bring to their bodies. They never tasted cooked food. And never imagined that there was a force out there that could bring light to the dark hallways in the depths of their caves.

With nothing much to be done in collaboration with time, patience was not a virtue on Sand Island. Patience was like a golden coin. If ever found on Sand Island, it would not have any value. Islanders had no reason whatsoever to be patient or impatient, as much as they had no reason to own gold. Yet, one can easily mistake the islanders' anxiousness for impatience. Like a mob of meerkats that rarely drift away from their burrows, islanders were constantly anxious. They were never free to wander away from their caves. They kept themselves close and around the cave entrances. They took turns gazing into the horizon and scouting the sky for signs of an approaching sandstorm or a treacherous tornado. They also took turns in their hunting and gathering missions. They were afraid of being far away from their shelters and facing a sudden tornado or a sneaky sandstorm in the middle of the night. Any islander who went out for a hunt had to keep sight of the cave's entrance. If a sandstorm or tornado struck, the islander should be able to dash towards the cave's entrance and away from Sand's blazing molars and its fatal stomach as quickly as possible.

There was a visible ancient mark carved on the entrance of their cave that was both comforting and terrifying to see at once. Scratched and eroded by Sand, the carvings were luckily still visible but not so deep. As children, they were curious and wondered who carved it, what it meant, and why it was left there. It looked like a shape that could not be seen anywhere else on Sand Island. Two mirrored triangles, one on top of the other, with their tips touching each other. The unfamiliar shape of a sand glass. All five islanders grew up and quickly lost their interest in the carving. They no more sought any answers to questions they once had. They grew out of the need for the meanings it carried. They were hungry and thirsty, and all they needed was food and water. Their hunger and thirst made the carved shape insignificant enough to disappear and blend into their rocky walls.

The five islanders lived in dark rooms four flights of stairs deep inside the caverns of the giant dark grey rocks. They breathed in the awful odour of urine and faeces; yet, the smell was still more comforting than the odourless dry land where Sand monsters roamed.

They had a few words to use or say, no words to read or write, and nothing to talk about. So instead, they poked each other and pointed at things that grabbed their attention when they were outside their caves and only used their names in the dark, away from Sand's sight. They feared calling out each other by their names out in the open. So their voices were strictly preserved for Sand.

They touched, cuddled, kissed, played, and occasionally had small fights, biting, pushing, and slapping each other. And no matter what, they never stopped singing.

All five were orphaned at a young age. Left alone with no huts, no tools, no clothes, no pots, and no stories. All that was left by the islanders' fathers and mothers were their scattered bones, fading memories, a few habits, and a few songs to be sung for Sand.

Those songs were the only survival instructions they had inherited from their parents.

* * *

It was the norm for mothers of Sand Island to pass the skill of sand-reading to their daughters. The mothers had always dominated sand-reading and song-singing. They were calmer than the fathers and more interested in keeping the tribe's harmony intact through their astute sense of the accord and tensions that tied and dismantled their tribe. Young mothers had acquired the skills that kept their babies and children alive. Old mothers further developed the skills that kept their tribe members alive. They kept the fathers sane and under control. They were also skilful in seduction and control of reproduction.

Fathers, on the other hand, were inferior labour. Either mad and dangerous or clumsy and playful. But, regardless of where a father stood within the spectrum of fathers, they were all cowards in the face of Sand, and they were all brought up to attend very well to the will of mothers.

Mothers ruled through a leading mother, a tribe chief, backed up by a council of mothers within the laws of the song. The tribe's chief commanded and consulted her tribe through song. She celebrated and alerted, charged and defended, motivated and punished with and through songs. Mothers used songs as the only true power and survival kit that led islanders to live long enough to experience the miraculous event of child-bearing. The songs were the chief's sceptre that was used to keep tribe members alive and protected from Sand.

Like their great grandmothers, they earned their power and their tribe's respect and trust through their songs. KaiKa had been fascinated by her mother's strength, mainly her power and authority. KaiKa's mother ranked other fathers and mothers as she pleased and distributed food and water as she deemed. No man or woman dared to stand against her. Even if an islander protested, all the other mothers and fathers defended KaiKa's mother while she stood with her head held high. For that reason, KaiKa paid full attention to her mother's lessons. She wanted to be just as strong and powerful as her mother.

KaiKa learnt when to sing, what to sing, and how to sing to Sand. Her mother taught her how to read sand and read her surroundings. Through a lifetime of practice, KaiKa learnt the skills of reading her tribe members and where to look for signs that would lead her to the next song Sand demanded.

Besides her mother's power and songs, KaiKa saw something more in her mother's eyes. Something special. Something she could not fully understand yet admired. At times when islanders ate the flesh of a deceased islander, KaiKa's mother allowed the feast but never participated. She oddly stepped away from the feast site and fought starvation alone. She gave her back to her starving tribe and mourned in solitude. KaiKa would spend time staring at her mother's tear-streaked face and wonder.

Though the islanders rarely felt guilt while feasting on a deceased fellow, it was not as rare as the cactus that seldom appeared on Sand Island. An islander would feel guilty when they came back empty-handed from hunting or when he stole food. Also, there was guilt when one sang the wrong song, causing a sandstorm or killing another islander. Shame, on the other hand, was rarer than guilt and felt and detected by a very few. On rare occasions when an islander might have felt shame, it was because they were terrible at hunting, useless, sterile, or weak. A woman might have also felt shameful if she did not have a voice to sing with. In KaiKa's mother's case, she always felt shame when she lost a tribe member to Sand and then felt shame from letting her tribe members feast on the deceased. While most islanders felt guilty for something they had done, only a very few felt shame about something they were forced to do or something they had not done. Guilt was publicly common and frequently visible on Sand Island, while shame was privately incomprehensible.

At an early age, KaiKa realized that there were more dunes and caves on Sand Island than they knew. Later, as she studied her mother, she also realized that there was more shame on Sand Island than the guilt they knew or felt. Only a leading mother would know how to unpack that invisible chest of shame.

KaiKa found her way to that invisible chest of shame the day she witnessed her mother crying while denying herself the right to break her fast with the flesh of NooaKhi's dead mother. Her mother had felt shame on losing one more dear islander to Sand. She had lost one more battle. She struggled to understand how she could ever negotiate with an enemy that was unwilling to meet halfway and make a truce.

Despite the many times KaiKa witnessed her mother lose against Sand, she still saw something in her mother's eyes that made her feel as if her mother were colossal and significant enough to stand against Sand.

To be as strong and powerful as her mother was not the challenge KaiKa struggled with. To be as divine as her mother was KaiKa's ultimate trial.

* * *

They sing for Sand while they hunt and eat,
and Sand dances while they sing, and taps its feet.
The more they sing, the finer the treat.
And if they ever dare to whine or bleat;
if they ever dare halt from singing songs of hunger,
Sand will be utterly upset.
It will send them all, forever in slumber.

* * *

The song of hunger kept the islanders from starvation as much as possible. They sang it while hunting for more prey; they sang it while they ate to regulate food consumption and avoid overeating. They sang it to calm their aching stomachs when starvation struck. It was the same song; yet, they sang it differently throughout the day with different purposes in mind.

On their hunting missions the islanders orchestrated a fast-paced song, using inhales and exhales as instruments and hunting tools that kept them focused and enhanced their coordination and collaboration. The hunt leader commenced the quest by initiating the song through deep and steady loud exhales to indicate the speed and tension of the chase. Other tribe members then amplified the song through contrasting loud inhales to indicate the direction of the prey, giving the rest of the group some sense of navigation. Islanders occasionally filled the song with ornamentations of mouthful blows of melodies to guide and cheer on each other. The song directed them when to sprint and jump on prey and alerted misguided members to stop fooling around.

The rewards of their hunts were far more precious than the food they came back with. They connected through hunts and bonded through play and work. They laughed. Sometimes they fought. But most of the time, hunting quests gave them the chance to impress each other with their skills. After their hunts, other rewards were the promotions they got from their chief; the higher rankings earned them more respect, and more food and water.

When the hunt was over, and while eating the islanders sang together another joyful variation of the song of hunger. A louder song that replaced all those sly whispers and tactical hunting blows. One islander would eat, and the rest would watch and sing while waiting for their turns. They sang, but their minds were always distracted by counting turns and food eaten. To take an islander's turn was unforgivable, and to eat twice as much in a single turn was intolerable. Thus, the song served as an economic system that regulated food intake and prevented overeating.

SeeKa would purposely and impatiently pick up the pace of this song to rush others while they ate so her turn would come faster. Her tribemates would, in turn, slow her down while breaking their melodies with laughter.

When the feast was done, the fun was gone, and there was no food stash to tame their hunger, they returned to the same song that fed them. Islanders would sing a third variation of the song of hunger to announce that the food they stored had perished. However, this time they slapped and tapped their bodies and heads and childishly slapped each other and used their bellies and foreheads to add percussions into the song. They pacified their angry tummies through the song and called for others to start digging into their stashes and share what they might have sneaked and hidden away for times like these. It was a call for the strong islanders among them to share what they had with the weak and the neediest.

KaiKa and her tribe used all three variations of the song of hunger to turn times of distress into times of solidarity and vivacity.

* * *

One night, the moon was up, almost complete and unusually bright. It was anticipating, looking down at the islanders, like a spectator waiting for the game to begin.

Sand was kind to allow a tiny bit of humidity to sneak into the island and cover its dunes like an invisible damp sheet of a blanket.

The sky was clear, and the five islanders could see the stars scattered across the black canvas of the night. Stars had no significance, though. And planets were not any different from the stars. They had no names and stories to tell and no enlightenment or counselling to offer. And no one ever was curious to notice if planets and stars aligned. They were all just there to shine in the sky, like the ocean waves were, just there, to remind the islanders that they could not touch anything that lay beyond the borders of Sand Island.

KaiKa sneaked out slowly in the moonlight, followed by LaKhi and NooaKhi. She walked consciously without leaving any footprints behind her. KaiKa's head leaned towards her path, and her pupils were wide open. Then, with a deep inhale, she commenced the hunt and whispered the song of hunger with a plodding tempo and melody, commanding others to scan the dunes and their horizon. As they moved forward, LaKhi was advancing on KaiKa's far-right. He joined the song and started a harmonious layer of breaths indicating that a sand mouse was in sight. On KaiKa's far left was NooaKhi, who crouched slyly by taking small footsteps. He too added rhythmic exhales and inhales of his own. His eyes were set on another sand mouse.

The blind young AiYi and the airy SeeKa had to stay back at their shelter in front of the cave's entrance, right under the mysterious carving. SeeKa kept her eyes set on the sky, looking for the slightest sign of a Sand monster—a tornado or sandstorm. The girls' task was to shout and scream as hard as they could whenever a sandstorm or tornado appeared, and through their voices, they would lead the two men and their chief to the cave's entrance.

KaiKa spotted the two mice LaKhi and NooaKhi were after. And for better coordination, she guided the young hunters by picking up her song's pace. When they got close enough to their sand mice, the two hunters and KaiKa blew their final tune. They rapidly sprinted and leaped over the defenceless sand mice. LaKhi swung his arm in the air and caught the sand mouse with his right hand before landing back on the ground, then kicked up and stood on his feet with his arms up high, holding the mouse with pride, like a trophy, and looking around to see if NooaKhi had seen his acrobatic trick. But then LaKhi tripped over and fell, trapping his mouse under his body. He giggled and slipped his hand under his chest to grab the mouse's tail and leg. The unfortunate mouse had almost escaped. The moon was waggish enough to make sure it passed KaiKa's frown to LaKhi through the humid darkness.

At that exact moment, silently and masterfully, NooaKhi sprinted further away from KaiKa and caught the second sand mouse without any mishaps. The two hunters stood off the ground, each with a sand mouse in hand. KaiKa dashed towards NooaKhi and slapped the back of his head while singing in anger. She pinched his lips commanding him to keep singing while hunting. It was taboo to hunt in complete silence. NooaKhi rubbed the spot on his head where KaiKa had slapped him. He did not witness LaKhi's pride, and LaKhi was busy witnessing NooaKhi's humiliation. Still, NooaKhi joined KaiKa's song with a sour look on his face. Then, the two hunters tuned towards LaKhi's new melody while they sprinted towards their third and fourth prey.

After each catch, the young men crushed the sand mice's skulls with their hardened thumbs and then handed over their trophies to KaiKa. She counted the mice and piled them on the ground where they would return once the chase was over.

The hunt went on for as long as the moon was up and entertained. LaKhi and NooaKhi went back and forth to KaiKa with mice in their hands. When the moon got bored and started to slowly fade away, KaiKa tied the tails of all the mice, held the knot, and stopped the song of hunger. She announced the end of the nocturnal hunt.

Besides the hungry islanders, there were other predators too that hunted sand mice. Like the starving little wolf snakes. They almost always spat out the dead mice. The islanders also hated those greedy snakes for being wasteful. And there were the sandstorms and tornadoes. The bullies kept snatching the mice off the ground but never ate them. They picked mice out of their burrows, lifted them in the air, and tossed them into the mouth of the greedy ocean. A bribe to keep the ocean as corrupt as ever.

But this was a great night. None of the Sand monsters were around to disturb the hunt. No witless snake was found around KaiKa's pile of mice. And not a single mouse managed to escape from the two great hunters, LaKhi and NooaKhi.

* * *

The triumphant hunters returned from their blissful chore to sand nests scattered close to their caves' entrances. They had been rewarded with three dozens of sand mice. This was enough food to keep them alive for thirty more days, should Sand decide to trap them in their caves again.

The five islanders skinned and eviscerated the sand mice using sharp rocks and whatever teeth they had in their mouths. The chief collected all the meat and made sure no one hid any meat in their hair or fists. Once KaiKa piled up all the food, she distributed the mice among her tribe: nine to LaKhi, six to SeeKa, seven to NooaKhi, and just one to AiYi, and kept the rest with her. It was usual for NooaKhi to get less than LaKhi, that was KaiKa's distribution. She only gave NooaKhi more mice at times when she wanted to humiliate LaKhi for something silly he had done or at times when she needed a favour from NooaKhi. KaiKa did not give AiYi more than one mouse to protect her from the one thief among them. SeeKa had a habit of stealing a mouse or two from AiYi, digging them somewhere, and storing them for herself. When caught by NooaKhi, she got a harsh scolding from the tribe. KaiKa aggressively punished SeeKa by biting her, leaving deep painful marks of her upper right incisor on SeeKa's hands and arms, causing SeeKa to cry all night. During that noisy night, LaKhi had attempted to comfort SeeKa, and KaiKa frowned at him and commanded him to stay away from SeeKa so she could learn her lesson.

Once the islanders got their share of meat from KaiKa, they sat on the ground in a circle and sang together the song of hunger. At the same time, each took their turn, tamed their grumpy impatient stomachs with a tiny mouse, and cured the rest using sea salt they gathered from salt formations on the shore. SeeKa was behaving well that night. She kept the song's pace unbothered.

After their meal, KaiKa led her tribe to their cave at dawn. She walked into a curtain of flies that had just woken up and then marched into the cave and down its deep throat.

AiYi was always the last to enter the cave and the first to reach its safest rooms. She knew where to walk, knew which rocks to avoid, and had learnt how to navigate through the cave's narrow hallways. After all, she was the master of darkness.

As all five islanders were walking in total darkness down to the pond at the heart of their cave, KaiKa stopped singing her song of hunger and prepared to sing the song of thirst.

* * *

Whenever the islanders passed by the grumpy sea, they sang the song of thirst for Sand to lead water droplets into their small ponds inside the caverns. They sang whenever they drank water and hoped that Sand would replenish their precious tanks. And they sang for Sand whenever they urinated, so the toxic astringent liquid could be transformed into pure water that would seep back up to the ground and reappear in their ponds as freshwater.

KaiKa and her fellow islanders were conscious of how horrifying thirst could be. The dryness, the dizziness, and the terrifying ghosts and visions they saw when they become too thirsty. Their fathers and mothers had treated water so sacredly. With the song of thirst, they passed on the elementary knowledge that life was possible and bearable only where there was water. Without water, their blood would dry out and they would all fall dead, one after another. Islanders were brought up to understand that the ruthless Sand had the power to command the skies to hold its rain, causing women and men and all other living beings of Sand Island to die out of thirst. Therefore, the islanders sang the song of thirst at times of peace whenever the sky was clear. And they would keep singing even when sandstorms darkened the sky and at times of siege. They just never dared to not sing it.

Unlike the steady ocean wave-like and fast-paced song of hunger, the song of thirst had no rhythm and could be as slow as the movement of a palm tree's shadow during a sunny, windless day. Conducted by their chief, islanders made the most ravishing songs of thirst through sounds that created a breath-taking harmonious aria that pleased Sand and made sandstorms and tornadoes float away, dancing way above the moon and the stars and out of the ocean's sight. And sometimes, islanders sang the song of thirst like lullabies that soothed Sand into a deep slumber, unbothered under the surface of the raging ocean.

Terrified from thirst more than hunger, islanders sang the song of thirst more than singing the song of hunger. And the more a song was sung, the more it had variations, not to bore Sand with predictable notes. Thus, making the song of thirst like a cloud that had mastered shape shifting. It was a song that was seldom sung the same way twice.

There were rules that islanders followed when singing the song of thirst: Do not break the harmony. Do not suddenly stop singing on the wrong note. And most importantly, do not be dissonant. If any of those rules were broken, an islander might wake Sand from its peaceful sleep. And if Sand was awake, dancing and balancing on its toe, a dissonant islander would make Sand trip over and fall. Sand would be either irritated or embarrassed and offended in all cases. For that reason, islanders spent their lives practicing with their voices and perfecting the right sound that harmonizes with the rest of their tribe members' voices. With practice, islanders were also expected to acquire great taste in melody progression and know when to stop and when not to stop singing a melody.

An islander who was continuously dissonant or had terrible taste in songs was at risk of being exiled or sentenced to death by Sand or other tribe members.

Beauty on Sand Island was heard, more than ever seen.

* * *

Without teetering, AiYi swung from one rock to another like a hummingbird, leading her tribe effortlessly in the dark, dancing and swinging from one wall to another, ducking away from the hanging boulders in cracks and salt sticks stuck on the cave's ceilings.

It was AiYi's favourite time of the day, the only time when she raced SeeKa and the men who all submitted their senses to the cave's darkness. AiYi was more like a shepherd leading her sheep into safe grounds to eat and drink when absolute darkness fell on them. However, AiYi still barely felt equal to her tribe members. She was still their stray pet.

KaiKa followed AiYi carefully, singing the song of thirst while her tribe echoed her vocals. KaiKa used her song like a rope to keep herself tethered to AiYi and the rest while they moved inside the cave's hallways. NooaKhi followed KaiKa. Then SeeKa, followed by LaKhi, who always slowed down to ensure that his clumsy love was safe, not slipping off, and not left behind.

Occasionally, SeeKa and LaKhi purposely stayed behind to steal a chance to touch each other, hold hands, breathe over their rough skins, and kiss and bite. KaiKa would notice the fade of their sounds and sing louder, directing her song to the two lovers instead of Sand. SeeKa was always first to leave LaKhi's arms out of embarrassment and fear from KaiKa, picking up her pace and pulling LaKhi into the depth of the caverns. After all, they had nothing but free time and darkness to hide in. They could fool around anytime later; the moment KaiKa slept, SeeKa thought.

When KaiKa reached the edge of the main pond, she dipped her foot into the cold, sombre water. She reached down to the pond's floor to check how much water Sand had gathered for the thirsty islanders. Above her knee, as she left it last time. She felt comfortable. Then, KaiKa sang the song of thirst in her loudest voice, as she waited for her tribe to reach the small freshwater pond. Echoes of KaiKa's song travelled through the cave's curvy passages and into its edges. It resounded from every direction as if the entire space inside the cave was an extension of KaiKa's lungs. At times of peace, the echoes of the song of thirst alone could cleanse the islanders' dry bodies, faces, nostrils, skins, and throats.

All five were standing next to each other, facing the pond. The young islanders could not see each other in the dark but felt their presence through the choir of the song of thirst. They waited for KaiKa's voice to soften, followed by the sound of KaiKa's hand immersing into the water and disturbing the pond's calm surface. It was the signal that they could now dip their hands into the pond and drink three handfuls of water. They did not count the dips out loud, yet the water that reached their throats rarely exceeded their quotas. Even in the heart of the dark, they knew that all eyes were on them. With every dip, they raised their hands above to show Sand how much they were about to consume, so Sand could replace it. Then, they wiped their faces and heads with the remaining water droplets in their hands before dipping again. They took turns drinking to keep the song alive. KaiKa drank first while the rest kept singing. Then, it was LaKhi's turn, then NooaKhi's, then SeeKa's, and finally AiYi's. No other song exposed their hierarchy better than the song of thirst and the ritual of drinking water.

Once the five islanders finished drinking, KaiKa decrescendoed and commanded all to stop drinking from the pond's water. After drinking and washing, the islanders then head to their dark spots in different carved corners of the cave and put away their cured sand mice meat below piles of rocks they used as personal safes, away from the water ponds and away from each other.

After that, they rested. Some went directly to sleep, while others spent some time engaging in lustful activities before sleeping.

Sand strikes
whenever Sand likes.
It takes no one's permission.
It makes no allowance for prediction.
Frightening at night and equally frightening under the sunlight.
Sand emerges in shapes that are grisly and makes sounds that are eerie.
Monstrous ghastly thunderous clouds that dive and roar.
Mountainous furious snails, sailing from the shore.
And enormous, rapidly twirling pine cones
that groan and moan like torn crones.
They pick rocks and toss stones.
Eat corpses and spit bones.
At any time Sand likes,
from any direction,
in any formation,
Sand strikes with aggression, and without permission.

As a toddler, AiYi had lost her sight, left ear, half of her head's skin, and half of her hair.

She had been crawling about alone out in the open. A sandstorm had struck them all in the middle of the night while AiYi's mother and all the other mothers were asleep inside the cave. The terrified mothers had not noticed that little AiYi was not among the children inside the cave.

Sand's fingertips were strong enough to carry AiYi and slam her into the red-eroded walls that surrounded the caves. Sand wiped the rocky wall with AiYi's face and head, then pitied and regretted what it had done, so begrudgingly it safely landed the startled toddler on a soft bed of sand in front of the cave's entrance. Alerted by her daughter's cries, AiYi's dauntless mother immediately picked up the young child, even as Sand tried to hold on to the older woman. It touched the mother's hand and tried pulling her into its gut, but luckily the mother fled from Sand. She ran down into the cave's darkness, passing by anxious fathers who were wildly busy burying the cave's entrance. At the same time, she wiped the blood from AiYi's eyes, face, and head.

AiYi and her mother were lucky that night. No islander was clever, strong, heavy, or reckless enough to survive a sandstorm's pull, yet both mother and toddler miraculously did.

Sand was not satisfied with the islanders' offering. A frightened little girl was not the prize Sand was after. Nor that Sand would be satisfied eating a cowardly father. Only eating a courageous mother or father could have calmed Sand down with satisfaction.

Sand touched AiYi's mother and liked the taste of her hand.

Sand touched AiYi's mother and liked the taste of her hand before she fled into the caves. Sand kept knocking on the gates of the cave in rage. It barked and shouted outside of the cave, demanding islanders to give away one of their bravest mothers or fathers.

That sandstorm lasted longer than expected. The islanders had started to run out of food. A mad hungry father known for his frequently random laughter approached the moaning sleeping AiYi in the dark. He woke her up and shocked her with his terrifying song of hunger. He held AiYi's head and lifted her in the air—her neck carrying the weight of her weak body. Her legs were hanging loose. She screamed and kicked in every possible direction. She almost broke her neck while wildly twirling as she swung her legs in the air. The father embarrassed her and locked her body into his. AiYi first smelled his warm repulsive breath approaching her face, then felt his thick bushy beard covering her face before he placed his large dry, scaly lips on her bloody right eye and sucked it out of its socket. At the same time, AiYi filled the caverns with deafening wails of immense pain.

AiYi's mother and two other mothers surged to the little girl's rescue. In complete panic and the darkness, they rumbled against each other, ran and banged their heads into a few ceilings, slipped and stumbled over rocks, and raced each other towards the child's sirens. Still, before they could reach the defenceless little girl in the dark, another hungry father had sucked out her other eye. Holding one of her legs, she was hanging in the air upside down and was crying in the dark. She was handed over to NooaKhi's mother, who immediately embraced the child. Soaked in blood, NooaKhi's mother checked AiYi's body and looked for any missing hands, fingers, or toes. She was not sure where to look anymore before she gently handed over the child to her own mother, who instantly noticed the void the mad fathers had left inside AiYi's eyelids. She screamed hysterically in terror and anger. All mothers, including KaiKa's, surrounded AiYi's mother to calm her down.

Later, AiYi's mother got the permission of the tribe's chief to wipe her daughter's face with water. Then, she sang the most beautiful song of thirst in the form of an aria, joined by the other mothers. She kept her weak, shivering child in her arms throughout that sandstorm, away from all fathers, like a lioness protecting her injured cub in a dark den filled with fuming hyenas.

Sand heard AiYi's mother's screams that night and immediately halted. Her screams vibrated with weakness. Sand was no longer interested in tasting the rest of the mother's body. A few days later, the islanders dug themselves out of their cave and went out to make the most of the lull. While all islanders went hunting, AiYi's mother headed directly to the salt formations seeking the ocean's healing powers. She soaked her daughter's face with burning salty seawater every dawn. She forced her daughter to look right into the eye of the sun until AiYi's eye sockets stopped bleeding and thoroughly dried. Her eyelids concaved in the void of her skull.

After several full moons, AiYi was healed entirely. However, she became blind, with a burnt scalp and frail legs that could barely carry her a few steps. She had not sung a song either. Nevertheless, AiYi developed a reputation among mothers as the little toddler that was strong and lucky enough to survive Sand and cave monsters.

Another sandstorm raided. This time, the sandstorm ate a dying mother before sending the rest of the islanders into their caves. Again, it lasted longer than expected, and the islanders' inventories of mice meat began to perish. A laughing mad father plotted to end the tribe's starvation. He sneaked in the dark and tried to seize AiYi right out of her mother's arms. Two other mad fathers joined him in the act and the laughter. The three laughing fathers believed that AiYi was too weak to survive the sandstorm, and they all wanted a piece of the prize. At the same time, all the mothers stepped in to save AiYi from the madmen. However, the tribe's chief instructed the other mothers not to interfere and avoid a total outbreak of war between the three laughing madmen and the last three fertile mothers on Sand Island. After all, losing one mother was wiser than losing all three.

AiYi's mother's persistence to keep her daughter alive forced her to go through a long deadly battle against the three laughing men. During the bloody battle in the dark, one of the mothers successfully snatched AiYi from the madness, while the laughing men hysterically kept beating

AiYi's mother. Finally, the brave mother became a martyr who sacrificed her life to save her daughter. The mother's body ended the starvation of the three laughing men and four other innocent children.

Shortly after that sandstorm, the three laughing fathers gradually lost their ability to move their legs and hands, then died. And the tribe's chief was committed to protecting the little child, in honour of the child's dead mother.

More than a dozen sandstorms later, AiYi, still a weak child, picked up a peculiar skill. She used the raging ocean waves and echoes to map her way around the island. She also used the sand and rocks beneath her feet to create paths that led her from the cave's entrance to the shore and back. She identified different spots based on the sand she walked over. Some areas were hardened by rain, while other areas were ploughed and softened by sandstorms. Although sandstorms and tornadoes kept changing the island's features from time to time and wiped out the paths that AiYi drew, her persistence and cartographic skills kept recreating fresh memories that helped her navigate the island. She had the full map of all the island's caverns imprinted in her mind. Every stone, every ceiling, every floor, every hallway, and every corner. The last surviving mothers and the other young tribe members admired her mastery. They were all committed to keeping AiYi alive. She became their beloved pet.

AiYi never saw the faces of those who laid their lips on her face and forcefully sucked her eyes out of her skull. Instead, she had a vague memory of what happened to her mother in the dark. Further, she lost most of her childhood memory. Still, she had never forgotten the terrifying song of hunger she heard before having her right eye sucked out of its socket.

Growing up, AiYi never caught any sand mice or other prey. She was prey once, and the same song that ended her hunger was once sung for Sand to lead the hungry fathers to her. AiYi continued singing the song of hunger, even though listening to her tribe sing as they hunted gave her the chills.

She still did not want to upset Sand, KaiKa, or the other three islanders.

AiYi found her comfort and peace in the song of thirst. The same song her mother sang on the night when AiYi lost her eyes. A song that her mother kept singing every time she soaked her daughter's eyes with healing seawater from a salt formation near the ocean. Still, with all the comfort AiYi got from the song of thirst, all songs of thirst were songs that also offered condolences to her grief.

Therefore, AiYi had to find another song that gave her the most comfort and peace, one that Sand Island could never offer. So, she sang another song that she kept for herself. While AiYi sang aloud the songs of hunger and thirst with her tribe, she also sang and murmured her own secret song in her head. She never dared to sing her song aloud. She was afraid KaiKa would not allow it.

Nonetheless, whenever KaiKa heard AiYi sing the song of thirst, she allowed AiYi to lead. After all, KaiKa was already grown enough to bleed like the other mothers when AiYi lost her eyes and mother. She could not help but feel ashamed for not stopping her laughing fathers from eating her eye. KaiKa always felt ashamed that her mother had allowed her mad-laughing fathers to attack AiYi and kill AiYi's mother. And she was guilty of accepting the flesh of AiYi's loving mother.

KaiKa knew that there was more than thirst in AiYi's songs. KaiKa, who also missed her own mother, found the love and warmth of a mother in AiYi's songs. So whenever KaiKa heard AiYi sing the song of thirst, she felt the desire to see motherhood shine on the island again.

AiYi's song of thirst made KaiKa want to sing the song of hope.

Chapter Two
Songs of Fear and Hope

Sand Island's inhabitants were all married to each other.

Incestuous lovemaking was common and essential. The islanders' survival depended on bearing children as much as they could.

They were all mothers and fathers to their children. After all, they could only be sure of who their mothers were but never certain of their fathers. Moreover, because breastfeeding was a public service, it was also possible for a few children to make several bonds with other mothers and grow up unsure of who gave birth to them.

LaKhi, NooaKhi, KaiKa, and SeeKa had shared fathers. But none of them were particular about who their father was, and it was never a point of interest. KaiKa and NooaKhi had special bonds with their own mothers and were certain of who their mothers were. SeeKa, however, was not sure of hers. KaiKa was old enough to witness and remember her own mother giving birth to SeeKa but could not tell any stories of it. And LaKhi, on the other hand, was never told that he was an orphan. Like SeeKa, he was breastfed and cared for by all living mothers.

Harmony was encouraged through fluidity and occasional foreplay across all tribe members. It was common for women to touch, peck, kiss, cuddle, and caress their bodies against men and other women. It was also common for men to sleep and cuddle and exchange favours with other men besides women. Love and childbearing, on the other hand, were only applaudable if approved and blessed by the tribe's leader and other mothers. The chief's songs regulated love among islanders and governed childbearing.

Pregnancy was dangerous on Sand Island and could only be initiated after a thorough assessment and careful sand reading. As much as they needed children for their tribe's survival, the tribe leader had to carefully read the harmony between Sand and the islanders, and take note of the unity among her tribe members before committing to the act of love. If pregnancy occurred without careful sand reading, Sand could end the life of the child and its mother. Even when pregnancies successfully and miraculously ended with a celebrative survival of the child and its mother, the odds of the child surviving long enough to walk were very slim. The defenceless children of Sand Island had to overcome too many unknown illnesses, starvation, and dehydration before they walked and sang.

Rape was almost forbidden. Intercourse by force, when approved by the leading mother, was not rape.

Strong fertile mothers were sacred, though not as sacred as Sand, but nearly as sacred. To harm a fertile, healthy mother by forcing her into love could exhaust her miraculous childbearing capacity. Hence, forcing a fertile mother into bearing a child was seldom allowed by a tribe leader. However, the punishment for rape was often benign.

Strong fertile fathers, who sang well, were scarce too. A strong father caught in rape would be punished by humiliation rather than violence. He would receive a lower rank in water drinking. He would also receive punishments through starvation. He would receive a lesser amount of food after hunting. Nonetheless, a strong fertile father could quickly reclaim his rank, too; a single good hunt, or a charming song, could easily earn him the respect he had lost.

Low-ranked, weak, sterile dissonant men, on the other hand, could be expelled by the leader. No father wanted to be banished and alone. It was considered a death sentence.

To live in exile meant that a father would not be allowed to share shelter and would have to face sandstorms in the open or inside the other rocks and caves of the island, alone. The punishment meant driving fathers to inevitable madness before feeding them to sandstorms and tornadoes. At the same time, no chief wanted to expel islanders. Banishing a father who could manage to survive sandstorms and tornadoes inside caves meant that he might live on rogue without paying attention to Sand's songs and consequently upset Sand and cause more harm on the island.

Politics in this matter were as simple as that. KaiKa imitated her mother's diplomacy and always thought twice before punishing NooaKhi and the others.

KaiKa had to bend the rules and norms to govern the last few islanders.

* * *

NooaKhi was born a big, brutal boy who had almost killed his mother at childbirth. He grew up, however, to be a huge boy living among tiny islanders.

By the orders of KaiKa's mother, NooaKhi, who had started walking and looked twice as old as he should, was denied access to breast milk so that KaiKa could have a chance at more nutrition before her mother's milk went dry. And by the time KaiKa weaned and walked, LaKhi took over NooaKhi's mother's lap and breasts.

Among the three older children, NooaKhi was the first to have a complete set of teeth. He was the first to run and jump, climb a rock, explore the shores, and join a hunt. He was a favourite among his fathers. They enjoyed playing with NooaKhi. They raced against him and wrestled him to the ground. He won a few times against his fathers and never stopped asking for more play with the fathers. They taught him all their wit and the games they knew and always asked him to perform new acrobatic tricks. Yet, he was a menace in the mothers' eyes, for he was the last child to sing before

AiYi. His first song was unrecognizable. His second song was barely recognized as a song of hunger.

Whenever NooaKhi attempted to play and wrestle against KaiKa, his mother would immediately interfere and stop him in respect of KaiKa's mother's wishes. She demanded that all should pay her daughter the respect of an heir, the respect a princess would deserve. KaiKa was untouchable and not supposed to be harmed or humiliated by any child, mother, or father. While KaiKa innocently played and threw sand, remains of corals, and shells at NooaKhi, he was not allowed to play or hit back. KaiKa would tease NooaKhi in front of the mothers and sneak a slap to his forehead, neck, or butt, and he would be denied the right to slap her back. And if he ever hit KaiKa in defence, he was beaten by his own mother and sometimes by other mothers, too. Beating children by fathers was not a norm among the islanders. It was cowardly of a father to hit a child no matter what. Only mothers were allowed to discipline their children if they had to, while fathers were there to strengthen all of them through hunts and play.

NooaKhi kept his childish acts of vengeance against KaiKa to the darkness of the caves. When mothers, fathers, and their children visited the water pond for drinking or were trapped by a sandstorm inside the dark caves, NooaKhi would creep in the dark and painfully pinch, kick, bite, or punch KaiKa and even hit her with a rock on the head. She would cry out loud in the dark and scream NooaKhi's name. However, the cave's darkness was not the proper setting for children's trials to be made. The mothers' appetite to punish a child was suppressed by the terror and anxiousness caused by the sandstorms and hunger. Besides, mothers had enough parental instincts to not scare a child in the dark. Accidents could happen, and a child could break a neck or a bone. Hence, NooaKhi would take advantage of the dark to rigorously and repeatedly give back KaiKa all the slaps she had lent him under the eyes of the sun. The cycle of harmful childish debt did not end but grew. The more harm NooaKhi traded back in the darkness, the more injury KaiKa traded back in sunlight and under the protection of the mothers. They were never fair in their trade and kept raising the stakes. Yet, they became loyal merchants, with ties knotted by hatred and jealousy.

Unlike KaiKa, LaKhi was never protected from NooaKhi's childish painful games. As old boys, NooaKhi and LaKhi always picked up fights over food and prey, over their sleeping and napping spots inside and outside the caverns. And whenever in battle with his half-brother, LaKhi always lost to NooaKhi's fist, weight, and suffocating arms. However, he was never a target of NooaKhi's harmful intentions. On the contrary, the two boys always played together like loving brothers.

NooaKhi grew to be the closest resemblance to their fathers. He grew a shorter temper than KaiKa and was easily carried away with anger. It was challenging to defeat him, and he was never as obedient as LaKhi. He did not readily submit to KaiKa's mother's authority. Though he had his fathers' temper, like his mother, NooaKhi was overprotective of his tribe. He was restless and did everything an islander could do to keep himself and his tribe alive and out of trouble. He always came back from hunting trips with the most amount of food. He always had his eyes wide open, looking for a trace of prey and watching the horizon for any signs of approaching sandstorms and unpredictable tornadoes. Whenever tornadoes or sandstorms did appear, NooaKhi was first to run and carry AiYi on his shoulders and whatever food they had out in the open. He was also the first to close the cave's entrance. And when tornadoes or sandstorms calmed down, he consistently outperformed his half-siblings in digging themselves out of their caves.

KaiKa's mother worried about NooaKhi's inability to participate in songs the way mothers expected. She was also concerned about his disrespect to her authority and, at the time, his disrespect for Sand's songs. The whole tribe, including NooaKhi himself, was aware of his inability to sing. Yet, he did not stop trying and constantly competed against his brother in song contests and always lost all the song battles he ever had. Moreover, NooaKhi would foolishly initiate songs at the wrong place, at the wrong time, or with a bad voice and tone.

By the time KaiKa grew into puberty and released blood, her mother worried that the mothers and fathers might not survive to witness the birth of their grandchildren. She stressed that KaiKa might soon become a mother without the guidance of an experienced mother to show her the ways of keeping a child alive and singing. Through her songs, she instructed KaiKa and NooaKhi into the act of childbearing. KaiKa resisted, then protested and rejected him. NooaKhi was the boy she hated the most. Too sneaky. Too angry. Too foolish. Too big. Had the ugliest voice. And was too disrespectful. She attested and pointed at his awful voice that could not sing. Yet, she had no other choice. KaiKa was afraid to seem like a foolish girl who did not adhere to her mother's wisdom and the will of Sand. She was afraid that her mother would stop teaching her sand-reading and turn her attention to SeeKa instead. KaiKa also feared bearing a child of a laughing mad father instead of NooaKhi's. And although LaKhi had a winsome voice, LaKhi was still singing with the stunning innocent voice of a sterile little girl. NooaKhi, on the other hand, accepted KaiKa's mother's instructions with pride and glory. Fathers were joking around him, giving him tips and instructions. They giggled, performed, and demonstrated the benefits of being aroused. He celebrated with the fathers all week long because he was part of KaiKa's mother's plans. He knew that whatever KaiKa's mother planned was to be respected by KaiKa. For once, he was entitled to some respect from the untouchable arrogant princess he hated the most.

And so, KaiKa was forced to have her first coitus with NooaKhi while surrounded and celebrated by mothers. Fathers and children stood by too, unashamedly watching, laughing, and giggling.

The first time KaiKa got pregnant with NooaKhi, she bled and miscarried in the darkness of the caves. The second time she got pregnant, she bled again and lost her child while running away from a sandstorm on her way to shelter. The third time she got pregnant, she gave birth to a dead unformed baby in the darkness of the caves. She was forced by her mother to eat her second and third babies in the dark. KaiKa marinated her own children's flesh with a condensed bitter taste of loathing towards NooaKhi.

The mothers consulted KaiKa's mother to amend her plans. They were all worried that Sand was raged and threatened by KaiKa and NooaKhi's offspring. They also stressed that KaiKa's body would become sterile by NooaKhi if the two foes made any further attempts. KaiKa's mother, who was convinced that NooaKhi fathering KaiKa's children could unite the two eldest children, was too embarrassed by her misreading of Sand. KaiKa's mother admitted that NooaKhi's dissonant voice was not worth the scandal and shame she might face. She instructed KaiKa to try LaKhi, whose voice by then had grown into the voice of a strong, fertile young man and was even more beautiful than before.

KaiKa was delighted to see her mother nodding to the mothers' wishes. However, KaiKa's body never responded to LaKhi's liquids. All of KaiKa's attempts to bear LaKhi's child ended with echoes of silence and rejection. While KaiKa believed that her body was ruined by NooaKhi's flesh and liquids, LaKhi believed his fluids were never destined to live and grow in any other body than SeeKa's. For his songs were all sung for her.

KaiKa stored the love she had carried for her unborn children in a chest and buried it. With every sandstorm and tornado, Sand slowly unearthed the chest and its contents. Some of the contents were passed on to AiYi, while KaiKa wore most of the chest's contents around her head like a crown that had beads dangling down to her neck, blinding KaiKa with grief. AiYi could have become a foster daughter if KaiKa did not hang on to her mourning accessories.

* * *

Mothers of Sand Island believed that the first Sand song sung by a child would forever be the child's omen. If a child's first song was the song of hunger, the child is deemed to be forever hungry and might grow up to be a thief or a good hunter, or both. If a child's first song was the song of thirst, the child will forever be thirsty and shall grow gullible and be easily manipulated by mirages, islanders, and sand, but could also grow up kind and giving. And if a child's first song was the song of fear, the child will grow a coward, forever afraid, forever chased by sandstorms and other phantoms; driven to madness and possessed by Sand, and ultimately turn into a monster. The song of hope was seldom a child's first song, yet, mothers believed that if it ever was a child's first song, the child would grow to be fertile or lustful. Mothers of Sand Island gave birth and raised nothing but doomed children, for all their children had not been fortunate to learn any other song but one of those four songs. Yet, they were lucky enough to sing because the mothers believed that a child who grew old and never sang a song would forever be labelled as cursed by Sand. A mute child was often segregated from other children, without food, weakened, and eventually starved to death. Hence, to sing the song of fear was perceived as a better omen by mothers than to pretend bravery through silence.

Mothers sang a simple short phrase of the song of fear whenever a child stumbled, slipped, or fell. Children then picked up the song of fear and sang it when they fell and cried in pain. Children, like their mothers, sang a repeated phrase in a high-pitched scream when a large wave hit the rocks on the shore, roaring and splashing. Like their fathers, children sang the song of fear in laughter when they sneaked up on each other at night or when a dead, skinned sand mouse moved and kicked. Horrified, the children sang the song of fear with their parents when thunder struck the island. Or, when the moon vanished for a moment in the middle of the night. Or, when the sun darkened while it sat right in the middle of the sky. Both moon and sun would fool islanders who thought that sandstorms had eaten the sky. And, of course, all children, mothers, and fathers sang the song of fear when sandstorms and tornadoes appeared. When afraid, the song of fear was the soothing remedy they needed. It brought courage to some and prepared others to face their definite death.

It was taboo to sing the song of fear for anything other than Sand. Nothing should be feared other than Sand. When they were children, their mothers smacked them whenever they slipped into the song for no good reason. So, they all had to grow out of the song and only reserve it for Sand and its monsters. It was also taboo to call an islander's name when singing the song of fear. A bad omen that could execute both, the one who spared a voice to shout the name and the bearer of the name.

Above all, no one dared to not sing the song of fear when it was sung by the tribe's chief. After all, it was the ultimate offense to not fear Sand.

* * *

SeeKa's father was a loner, an islander who lived far away from the tribe and sang his songs alone. KaiKa's mother seduced SeeKa's father, hoping she could keep him in her tribe, make use of his strength and protect her tribe from Sand raids he caused due to his unpredictable songs. However, SeeKa's father was unreliable and still too hard to predict. He threw food into the sea and buried some to rot elsewhere where no one could ever find it. He urinated in small ponds of freshwater. He threw sand at other sleeping islanders and rocks at lovers whenever he saw them embracing each other. Finally, he was expelled from the tribe for all the trouble he brought. And, as SeeKa's mother had predicted, he was ultimately lifted and struck down and away by one of Sand's ferocious tornadoes. Sand took its justice for all the annoyance he caused. After four full moons since SeeKa's father's death, KaiKa's mother gave birth to SeeKa and left her baby daughter to be raised and taken care of by other mothers. SeeKa's first song was a whiny song of hunger.

Growing up, SeeKa never showed much interest in anyone before KaiKa's second pregnancy. She was a quiet little girl who always played alone and away from KaiKa and the boys. While children slept together, kicked, spooned, and piled on top of each other, SeeKa was capable of sleeping alone. She found her peace and long tranquil sleep away from the other children. During sandstorms, SeeKa was calmer than the other young islanders. She was the least to whine. Except during songs of hunger and thirst. She begged for more water and food, and she whined louder than all the other children. And whenever drinking and eating ceremonies were over, SeeKa swiftly resumed her stealth. Mothers thought of her as an odd little girl. The 'quiet creeper' was a unanimous nickname that mothers never gave to SeeKa.

LaKhi once spotted little SeeKa creep into the sleeping spot of the fathers. LaKhi saw her steal a couple of mice from a stash the father hid under a large oval plate of rock. He quietly followed SeeKa out into the open and saw her unload her chest of rocks where she hid more stolen mice beneath the rocks. LaKhi was not as quiet as SeeKa. He stepped over a wiggling rock and made noise enough to expose himself. SeeKa, embarrassed, quickly covered her stash of stolen mice with her hands. LaKhi, however, smiled at her and assured her that he would carry her secret. She took one piece of meat out of her stash, tore it in half, and handed him half a mouse. Despite LaKhi's acknowledgement of her habit, SeeKa kept her habits and did not show further interest in LaKhi.

SeeKa was still a little girl when KaiKa lost her first child. Little SeeKa had no memory of KaiKa's first miscarriage. She had heard her sister cry and moan for long and assumed it was the work of NooaKhi in the dark. She was then quickly distracted by AiYi's screaming and continuous crying and moaning throughout that particular sandstorm.

SeeKa, however, always remembered KaiKa's second pregnancy. Her older sister's stomach was oddly growing. She learnt that her sister was carrying a child and was fascinated by the idea. Islanders grow inside girls before they come out into the open. Islanders lived in caves away from Sand before being born.

For the first time, SeeKa was interested in someone else, other than her own shadow. She followed KaiKa everywhere she went. Like a parasite, SeeKa repeatedly touched her sister's growing belly and did not care how much of an irritation she was to KaiKa who consistently slapped her little sister's hand away.

Then, once during a dry, dull day, fathers were spotted running towards the cave's entrance, shouting and alarming mothers and children of an approaching sandstorm. Everyone scattered in panic, digging out their food, and running for shelter. SeeKa, who was sleeping next to her older sister, was woken by the islanders' sound of terror and songs of fear. She woke up to KaiKa's face sobbing and howling. SeeKa then noticed blood dripping from KaiKa's body. Tracing the flow of her sister's blood, SeeKa was shocked to see a tiny dead baby on the ground. KaiKa's mother appeared and quickly picked up the tiny baby, held KaiKa's arm, and ran towards the cave. SeeKa was left on her own in shock.

LaKhi then appeared, carrying dozens of mice close to his chest. He stood in front of SeeKa, whose eyes were still gazing into the ground where the tiny baby was. LaKhi pushed SeeKa with his body. She moved absentmindedly backwards with slight resistance. LaKhi persistently steered her into the cave's entrance. The two young islanders got into the cave on time, right before it was shut firmly by NooaKhi and the fathers.

Throughout the sandstorm, LaKhi did not leave SeeKa alone. He fed her more than half of his food. He walked her to the pond when the islanders gathered to drink, and he made sure she drank. He sang her all the songs a mother would sing to a child. He was tirelessly taking care of her from the moment she woke up until she slept. And while AiYi's mother wrestled the laughing fathers for her life and cried for help, LaKhi wrapped his arms tight around SeeKa and whispered a calming song of fear into her ear. Finally, after the long deadly battle, and after several long days and nights of sleep and naps, the two children were awakened by the mothers. They were led together to see the light again and gnaw at what remained of AiYi's mother.

SeeKa clung to LaKhi ever since, and he never left her alone. LaKhi's shadow became the unanimous nickname that KaiKa, NooaKhi, mothers, and fathers never formally gave to SeeKa.

Unlike KaiKa, SeeKa grew up and did not show further interest in the well-being of her tribe members except LaKhi. SeeKa was obedient to her half-sister's authoritative protectiveness. Yet, she was the assertive and superior one when alone with LaKhi. In her mind, SeeKa was the leader of her tribe of two. She was a menace and constantly plotted her moves to test LaKhi and seek his affection and kindness. Whenever she went on hunts with LaKhi, she put on an act and pretended to be tired or clumsy or falling out of luck when catching her sand mice, only to see if he cared enough to share his prey. She pretended to limp when scouting for mice after a sandstorm, only to see if he was kind enough to carry her around. She strolled on purpose, only to see if he cared about her enough to slow down and check on her. She pretended to be drowsy, only to test if he would show more energy while entertaining her. She thwarted against his sprints when hunting to see if he would ever lose his temper. He never did. Even better, he would let her lay her head on his belly. She had many tricks that could steal LaKhi from NooaKhi and her half-sister's sight, and she was never ashamed of practising any of them at any moment. When all islanders sang songs of hunger and thirst, SeeKa blocked out everyone from her mind and sang a duet with LaKhi alone instead. And whenever she touched herself in the darkness of the caves to push away her anxiety from Sand monsters that kept them in captivity, she did so with LaKhi's hands in her mind.

SeeKa took on her mother's features. Her face was like a set of four full moons. Prominent round cheeks that connected her rounded forehead to her rounded chin. In between, her fat dry lips sat below her small blistered nose, almond eyes and thick short eyelashes, and fluffy eyebrows. Young SeeKa was slightly taller and prettier than her older half-sister, with fewer scars, more teeth, and less facial hair. Yet, SeeKa always assumed that she had many faces but not KaiKa's mother's face.

When KaiKa lost her second and third children, SeeKa became fearful of the idea of pregnancy. And when KaiKa failed to become a mother to LaKhi's children, SeeKa gloated and was glad to see that LaKhi did not become a father to someone else's child.

* * *

All islanders that ever saw KaiKa's face thought that she resembled two of the fathers. She had their broad foreheads, large funnel noses, oddly large curved jaws, tiny mouths, and sleepy uneven eyes. The two fathers were also fearless, thoughtless, short-tempered fools. However, as a young girl, KaiKa assumed that she had her mother's face. Water ponds were murky and matte, and there were no shiny surfaces on the island that could have proved her wrong.

During her mother's lifetime, KaiKa mimicked her mother's mindfulness. She remained as calm and stately as her mother when she dealt with other mothers and the fathers. A leading chief, KaiKa learnt, should not show her anger. Instead, a leading chief should express her rage and execute her violent decrees through her alliances.

Though she had more than three unborn grudges towards NooaKhi, KaiKa kept him close enough to her for him to feel the warmth of her body. She held him sleeping next to her to maintain an alliance and sustain more power and authority.

After her mother's death, KaiKa did not allow her tribe to eat her mother's flesh. To KaiKa, they were not worthy of tasting her mother's meat. Yet, simultaneously, the young islander felt relieved. Eating an islander's flesh only satisfied the mad among their fathers, KaiKa thought.

The day after KaiKa's mother's death, SeeKa, NooaKhi, and LaKhi went out for a hunt. They were still distracted by their grief and mourning for KaiKa's mother. They were too headless to scout, sneak, and crawl. They were too heavy to sprint and leap after mice. The three islanders came back from a hunt empty-handed. KaiKa was not pleased. She was unforgiving. She yelled and threw sand at NooaKhi. She frightened LaKhi and ran after him. When KaiKa failed to catch LaKhi, she hysterically and viciously bit SeeKa's earlobe. SeeKa wrestled and struggled. She tried to smuggle her ear out of KaiKa's jaws. As KaiKa tore her sister's earlobe off her head, the young islanders saw the faces of their frightening laughing fathers resurrect on the surface of KaiKa's face.

KaiKa went through many sleepless nights. She mourned her mother but could not spit the flavour of SeeKa's earlobe out of her mouth. She was visited by haunting memories of her fathers' madness and laughter. She dug deeper into her memories; she wanted to find a single memory of her mother biting someone's ear or shoulder. But she could not find what she was looking for. Her mother was calmer and too wise to run and chase any of the fathers. KaiKa started to doubt that she ever had her mother's face.

Few days later, SeeKa got used to the new shape of her earlobe. At night, AiYi accidentally stepped on KaiKa's leg while she was sleeping in the dark. KaiKa woke and kicked the little blind girl a dozen times. KaiKa kept kicking until she was stopped by her brothers. She regretted, diverted, and led her tribe and sang the song of hunger before they all had a meal. Then spent a few nights awake. The bruises on AiYi's thigh reminded KaiKa of AiYi's innocent face in pain as she laid down on the ground after getting kicked a dozen times.

That week, SeeKa was sleeping when KaiKa and the boys had returned from a hunting quest. KaiKa pulled SeeKa's hair and dragged her to the ground, then sang the song of hunger, and they all had a feast. SeeKa was relegated that night and got fewer mice than her usual quota. After two full sleepless nights, KaiKa compensated SeeKa with two mice.

A few days later, LaKhi mistakenly blocked KaiKa, who was chasing after a sand mouse, causing KaiKa to lose sight of the mouse. KaiKa shoved LaKhi to the ground and yelled at him, then sang the song of hunger and resumed the hunt. KaiKa later, apologetically, handed over one more mouse to LaKhi when she distributed mice meat after the hunt.

NooaKhi yawned while KaiKa sang the song of thirst around the pond inside the cave. KaiKa slapped NooaKhi's head and denied him the right to drink water that day. Then, she slept next to him and allowed him to mount and thrust his body against hers. She hardly hit LaKhi. He always outraced her when she ran after him whenever she felt offended by him. She had to sneak up on him in silence if she ever wanted to punish and beat him. At times, she would not even try to run after him and only spare him with a spiteful gaze and barks full of spit. He would show his respect, obey her, follow her instructions, and sing his way to earn her forgiveness. He always won her heart back with his voice and songs.

LaKhi was KaiKa's favourite half-brother. He calmly slept in her arms if he was not in SeeKa's. He was always gentle to AiYi. He shared his food with AiYi, often held her hand, and played with her gently in the open. LaKhi cared for SeeKa and AiYi and was obedient to KaiKa. He looked like his mad-looking hideous fathers but had the most enchanting sound among the five remaining islanders. LaKhi's mother had died young, right after his birth, and NooaKhi and KaiKa's mothers had cared for him. While NooaKhi's mother breastfed LaKhi, he was protected by KaiKa's mother from starvation and the starving laughing fathers.

LaKhi's voice was not the only remarkable quality KaiKa found in him. When KaiKa felt rage, she sang to calm down.

And LaKhi was always the first to sing with her. KaiKa believed that he truly understood the songs better than the rest of the tribe. Despite his disappointing lack of interest in sand-reading rituals, he still demonstrated strong Sand song instincts. He anticipated KaiKa's signals, tones, and melodies with accuracy and had excellent intuition. She felt that he was the only one to initiate Sand songs at the right time and place. LaKhi must become a father to SeeKa's children, she thought. He could steer SeeKa into motherhood. The two could revive the mothers' alliance KaiKa needed on Sand Island. With LaKhi's good grasp of Sand song and SeeKa's good grasp of LaKhi, their children could sing like their father and protect the tribe from Sand. Hence, KaiKa always kept LaKhi close to her, in the second rank.

On the other hand, SeeKa's lack of affection for NooaKhi was alarming. Mothers, KaiKa learned, were primarily dependent on foreplay and lovemaking to promote connection, unity, and survival of her kind. Therefore, KaiKa disapproved of her half-sister's romantic decisiveness and deemed it a foolish act affecting the tribe's harmony and security. KaiKa wanted to raise SeeKa to become like their mother. She bore children from different men to protect the tribe rather than selfish love.

KaiKa knew that she did not share a face with her mother whose fertility was also superior to her. The multiple failed attempts at childbearing and miscarriages would forever be an unwanted badge that would remind KaiKa and her half-siblings of how inferior she was to her mother. Still, KaiKa was determined to use SeeKa's fertility to replace her own infertile body.

To win back NooaKhi's complete obedience, KaiKa planned to make him a father.

But KaiKa could not offer NooaKhi AiYi's small fresh body or her half-sister's body. She knew well how painful NooaKhi could be and how the pain he caused could ruin a mother's body. Therefore, KaiKa planned that SeeKa should bear a child or two from LaKhi. Labour and experience could prepare SeeKa's body to bear NooaKhi's large children, KaiKa thought. Once SeeKa gave birth to four or five children from the two men, they would grow into fathers, and songs on Sand Island would be sung forever. This is what KaiKa hoped.

* * *

KaiKa woke up at night while the others were sleeping. She felt her mother's presence around the cave. She walked out of the cave looking for her mother's corpse. It was customary to lose the islanders' bodies after a single sandstorm. Sand always carried bodies and tossed them back as bones. At times Sand tossed the bones into the ocean and sometimes buried them beneath the dunes. Perhaps she could find a skull, she thought.

Walking carefully in the open and risking her life against sudden tornadoes and death, KaiKa was haunted by her behaviour against her tribe members. She was haunted by all the kicks and bites she had carelessly given to SeeKa and AiYi. She was also haunted by the thought of wearing her fathers' faces, instead of her mother's. She felt the need to touch her mother's face to compare it with her own.

She walked under a half-full moon. Her pupils were wide, and her skin was alert. She walked onto the beach, dipped her feet into the wet sands, and walked along the shore looking for a swollen corpse and bright white bones. The ocean was calm enough to allow her to walk on its edges. The ocean was staring at her, and KaiKa was careful enough not to look straight into the ocean's eyes. Her head was bent down in shame and fear, her eyes were focused and fixed on her feet. Her toes were scouting, longing to touch anything that was not water, sand, shells, or rocks.

KaiKa kept walking all night, and there was no sign of the sun yet. She was now far away from the cave. So far that she would never have a chance of running back if Sand decided to strike. She had reached parts of the island that she had never dared to visit before. She only hoped that if she turned around and kept the ocean to her left side, she could recognize the beach in front of her cave. Then she realized how she had passed through many beaches that looked exactly like the beach she knew. Turning and walking back would not help KaiKa find her beach at night. Only the sun now could guide her back home. It was too late to turn around. KaiKa kept walking.

The ocean was still looking. It slowly exhaled a humid breeze, then inhaled a dry one.

KaiKa's walk finally came to an end. A big rock blocked the path along the shore. One of the many limbs the giant rocky beds had. The rock's neck reached into the sea and dipped its head into the ocean. KaiKa climbed the slippery rock and reached the back of its dry neck.

There she was. Her mother's body. Unswollen and untouched. Perfectly preserved and laying down with her head looking up at the sky.

KaiKa knelt and touched her mother's face. She then touched her own. She was sure now. KaiKa had her mother's face.

Suddenly, the breeze froze, and the ocean stood still. Nothing around her made a single sound. Sand is coming, KaiKa thought. Sand is here.

A sound appeared from the depth of the ocean. A song. KaiKa recognized the voice of her mother, but could not recognize the song she was singing.

The song climbed up the rock, walked over its neck, and was as clear and near to KaiKa as her mother's body.

KaiKa's mother was instructing her daughter. She must keep singing. She must not fear Sand. She must not lose her mother's face. She must keep her tribe alive. She must provide and be just. She must guide SeeKa into motherhood. She must guide LaKhi and NooaKhi into fatherhood. She must guide AiYi into adulthood. She must stand strong against Sand.

The song blurred and stopped. The ocean moved again. Waves stirred the air and splashed. Droplets of the ocean poured over KaiKa's face and covered her body. KaiKa could not see her mother's face anymore. She panicked. KaiKa leaped to the edge of the rock and climbed down. A wave splashed over the rock and hissed with violence. KaiKa slipped off the rock and landed on her back over sand and other small rocks. Without paying attention to her pain and injuries, she got up and ran. She kept a small distance away from the sea. The sea chased her, roared, and splashed. KaiKa was soaked. She could not feel her own hands. She could not feel her knees and feet. She lost her sight. It was dark. KaiKa screamed.

She opened her eyes and saw LaKhi's face. He held her cheeks. SeeKa was behind him trying to get a look at KaiKa's face.

KaiKa looked around. She did not leave the cave. She did not find her mother. It was the works of a dream, KaiKa thought. It was a vision that only comes to mothers.

I must keep them alive, KaiKa remembered. I must keep singing, she asserted.

* * *

A few days after a successful hunt, KaiKa crawled out of the cave and walked into the open to watch the sand and the sea. AiYi silently followed in her footsteps while the other three islanders slept inside.

The sea was raging and whipping its waves at KaiKa and AiYi, warning them from coming close to its body. The wind was pitiful and gentle, and the sun stared down at KaiKa and AiYi in awe. The yellow flying sand travelled across the island's dunes, while sand reflected the sun's face in every direction. The entire island was fluttering like a massive piece of golden silk. The flying sand was not easy to see or follow, but it was easy to fall in its hypnotizing force.

KaiKa stood there between the shore and the cave, observing her surroundings and reading the sand, humming a song her mother used to sing in her mind. A song so close to her heart. One she did not want to forget.

Sand has been oddly gentle on the tribe lately. Three full blissful moons have passed since they last saw a roaring Sand monster approach. Even the last sandstorm was merciful. It only trapped the islanders for a few nights before it released them and allowed them to enjoy the graceful face of a full moon again.

KaiKa crouched then knelt on the ground with her head immersed right into the thin layer of the flying sand. She was kneeling perfectly on her four limbs with a straight body and her bottom pointing to the sun as if she had a scorpion tail and was ready to attack. Her face pointed right against the stream of the wind. She closed her eyes.

AiYi crouched next to KaiKa, humming her own song in her mind.

KaiKa cleared her mind from all thoughts and songs. Then, she waited for the discomfort in her legs, arms, and hips to numb and evaporate into the air. She waited for the sounds of the sea waves to fade out of her mind. Only then, when she cleared her mind from all the unwelcomed distractions that poked her body and danced in circles around her, she was able to focus her attention on the sand that flew directly into her dry, dusty face. She carefully felt every tiny pebble and particle collide with her face. She rigorously registered every collision in her mind. She registered every piece of information sand delivered to her face. How solid and how gentle each pebble was. How many pebbles hit her cheeks? And how many struck her forehead. For how long did some stick to her lips? How many fell off her eyelashes? How dense and dry was the air that carried the sand? She kept reading the sand, and every single pebble.

KaiKa was there alone, standing face to face in front of Sand.

She was looking for answers.

She read. Monsters? Mad?

A large grain hit her left eyelid. And she read. Not mad.

A small pebble got stuck next to the mark, the large grain left on her left eyelid. She smiled.

KaiKa shook her smile off her face in fear of getting distracted by the sand or misreading it.

A particle hit her curved nose tip. She read. Far? Sleeping?

A tiny grain slammed into her forehead and stuck there for a moment before it was hit by another pebble, and both fell off her face. And KaiKa read. Sleeping. Far, far away.

Finally, she read. Hope? Fear?

A large pebble hit her upper lip, shaking and struggling not to smile. And she read. Hope.

KaiKa then granted her smile the permission, and courage to appear and grow. She shook the sand off her face, opened her eyes, stood up on her feet, and rubbed her palms several times before noticing that AiYi was frozen next to her, shivering in fear.

While crouched next to KaiKa and facing the wind, the sand grains touched nothing on AiYi's face other than her eye sockets. AiYi felt the presence of a phantom. AiYi sang the song of fear. KaiKa rushed and held AiYi's mouth, commanding her to stop at once. Do not wake up Sand, KaiKa frowned. KaiKa would usually take offense if an islander sang the wrong Sand song. KaiKa remembered her mother's face. She wiped her frown, smiled, then hugged AiYi. She held the little blind girl's hand and led her back to the cave.

LaKhi and NooaKhi were awake and standing next to the cave's entrance and saw KaiKa and AiYi coming back from the beach. KaiKa was smiling. She passed by NooaKhi, kissed LaKhi's forehead, then returned to NooaKhi, and kissed his forehead too. Then went down to the cave. They both looked at her suspiciously. NooaKhi noticed AiYi standing still in the open, shivering and hiding the terror that grew in her chest and knees. He went closer and examined her. He touched her arm. AiYi startled, stepped back, yelled, then rushed into the cave's darkness.

NooaKhi looked at LaKhi and passed an unspoken question to his younger brother, who had no answers to share back. They had not seen KaiKa smile this way since her mother's death and never saw AiYi shiver next to a smiling KaiKa. LaKhi shrugged and carried on his chore, leaving NooaKhi alone in his muddle.

* * *

Later at night, the tribe cautiously took a break, enjoying an undisturbed quiet night out in the open. The moon was no longer full, yet it was graceful enough to shed some glow on the edges of their bodies and faces. The clouds were completely absent from the sky's fields, mysteriously hiding behind the horizon. The bystander stars were squinting and gazing at the islanders in silence, more curious and perceptive than usual. As the stars gazed down and brightened the sky, the ocean gazed right back at them. The breeze carried salt and a small pitiful offering of goodwill from the grumpy sea.

LaKhi shared cured sand mouse meat with SeeKa on top of a large rock next to the ancient carving. He was stripping delicate pieces of meat out of the tiny mouse bones and passing them to SeeKa as if he was passing dark pink flower petals. As KaiKa was singing the song of hunger, she hummed her favourite song in her mind and looked at the two young lovers. AiYi and LaKhi sang together with KaiKa while SeeKa nibbled on her small petals of mouse meat. NooaKhi sang too. However, his eyes were set on AiYi.

When SeeKa finally finished eating, KaiKa paused her song of hunger and looked at her half-sister, whose thighs were firmly entangled into LaKhi's thigh. After that, KaiKa froze her gaze into LaKhi's eyes. He was still singing a gentle song of hunger. SeeKa was entirely mesmerized by LaKhi's face and voice; she was like still water behind a rock in a streaming river, untouched by the passing white water forces.

After a long pause, AiYi stopped singing and looked up, swinging her head right and left, wondering why KaiKa's voice had stopped and what KaiKa's next directive song would be. Then, finally, KaiKa broke her silence and started to rub her palms, creating a steady rhythm. Then with excitement, KaiKa sang aloud the song she had been humming all day since the morning and during her sand-reading rituals on the beach. It was a song sung more frequently among their mothers but never sung since KaiKa's mother sang the song to KaiKa and LaKhi on the day they had coitus. KaiKa sang the song of hope for the first time since her mother last sang it. Mothers rubbed their hands when it was time to make children and rubbed their hands again when babies were born.

SeeKa and the two men, in an instant, raised their heads and looked at KaiKa, who had a big warm smile. A smile they have not seen on their chief's face before. Islanders could mistake the song for a few other occasions. However, the hand rub was unmistakably recognized by SeeKa, LaKhi, and NooaKhi.

Sand reading predicted that it was time for their tribe to bear a child, KaiKa announced while rubbing her hands. She revealed that they were ready to be mothers and fathers to new young islanders. She sang and declared that Sand was smiling at them and had sent them a peaceful message that carried a brief moment of truce. The clueless AiYi joined KaiKa, trying to sing along to a song that she had never understood when and why adults sang. AiYi miserably echoed the song of hope.

While KaiKa's song revealed that Sand was granting islanders the necessary peace to bear a child, AiYi's shivering voice claimed otherwise. NooaKhi saw that AiYi suggested that Sand was hiding its true intentions. NooaKhi now feared that KaiKa was leading islanders into a trap set by Sand. He feared that Sand was after SeeKa and her unborn children.

LaKhi, on the other hand, was getting as excited as KaiKa. It was the night he had been waiting for. As SeeKa read KaiKa's prediction, ghastly memories of KaiKa's second miscarriage came back like a phantom that hid in the cracks of the grey mountains, nibbling on the remains of KaiKa's last unborn child. It had returned to haunt SeeKa again. She looked into KaiKa's eyes, then LaKhi's, and back to KaiKa. SeeKa resisted.

LaKhi saw the moon reflecting on SeeKa's face. Then, he started to rub his palms and sing with KaiKa. His voice was deep and heavy enough to pour masses of air and stir the water surface of the ponds deep in the heart of the cave. LaKhi transitioned KaiKa's plain song with his vibratos. He rubbed his hands, and through his song, he reached out to the moon and rubbed its cheeks.

KaiKa walked towards the two lovers, held their hands, kissed both hands, and she walked them to the cave entrance. Then, she released their hands, placed her own hands on their backs, and gently pushed the two lovers. Next, KaiKa pointed to the same spot her mother had once led her to. A bed of sand next to the cave's entrance. She commanded SeeKa to sing and make love on that spot. NooaKhi cautiously followed and examined. LaKhi sang, but SeeKa did not.

With their hands tied, the two lovers looked at each other. SeeKa was not sharing LaKhi's excitement. She was still hesitant. She always wanted LaKhi but did not want to have an islander grow inside her body. She was afraid of the life-threatening damage a baby could cause to her.

KaiKa stepped in and closer to SeeKa. She smiled at her. Held her hand and crouched, urging SeeKa to sit. SeeKa froze and did not bend a knee. KaiKa's smile faded. She stood up, still singing, and faced SeeKa. She was now commanding SeeKa to sing. NooaKhi and LaKhi felt the change in KaiKa's tone. SeeKa started to sing. AiYi and SeeKa's shivering voices were losing the battle against LaKhi's carefree deep beautiful voice. They were also losing against KaiKa's assertive authoritative song of hope. The two little girls' song of hope wanted to transform into the song of fear but was not allowed to.

Despite KaiKa's wishes for the two lovers to use her old bed, LaKhi took SeeKa down into the cave; they had their own bed. KaiKa was displeased when they ran away. She wanted to celebrate their love the way mothers did. But she let them go.

When KaiKa came out of the cave, she saw NooaKhi standing next to the sand glass carvings and holding hands with AiYi whose shivers were now more pronounced than earlier in the sunlight. AiYi murmured a song of fear. KaiKa came close to NooaKhi and AiYi and heard AiYi's song of fear. She instantly pushed NooaKhi away, held AiYi's shoulder, and shocked her violently. She commanded her to stop singing the song of fear. The little blind girl stopped and wailed. KaiKa slapped her and demanded she stops crying. AiYi sniffed and swallowed her breath. Then, KaiKa started to sing the song of hope again, and AiYi sang with KaiKa a broken song of hope.

NooaKhi, surprised, stood there like a breathing shadow with two glowing eyes now casting pale anger. Pretending to be unbothered by his silence and the glare in his eyes, KaiKa moved towards NooaKhi with a smile on her face and did not stop singing. Still, NooaKhi fixed his eyes on his sister's face. The tip of KaiKa's smile now lost its balance. NooaKhi lowered his head and closed his eyes, only showing his angry forehead. KaiKa held NooaKhi's chin and raised his head while still singing. She noticed his fear. Through her eyes, KaiKa tried to calm down NooaKhi and asked him to join her song. She softened the tone of her song.

KaiKa was now worried that NooaKhi's silence would offend Sand. She believed that Sand would curse the night, scare the moon away, and paralyse the breeze. Her half-brother's blasphemous silence would break the truce Sand had made and would not grant the islanders the hope they were seeking.

NooaKhi, on the other hand, was worried Sand was already offended. AiYi and SeeKa's shivering suggested that the night was already cursed by Sand. He feared that KaiKa's mother had chosen the wrong chief. He believed that KaiKa's sand reading was nothing more than a means for KaiKa to do what she pleased, and not what Sand desired.

NooaKhi was questioning KaiKa's songs.

NooaKhi respectfully lowered his head again and tried to

hide his scepticism from KaiKa. Still, KaiKa forcefully lifted his chin and switched her soft tone with an assertive one. She needed his allegiance. NooaKhi pulled his jaw away from KaiKa's fingers and turned his back in silence with his eyes open and reddened by anger, fear, and tears. He walked a few steps away and stood facing the cave.

KaiKa turned to AiYi, whose song was dominated by her shiver. KaiKa thought of AiYi's terrified face back on the beach earlier, and the sand in AiYi's eye sockets. KaiKa felt a sudden rush of disgrace. Her old worries were now replaced with fresh ones. Sand might have never made a truce. She might have made an irreversible error. She had misread Sand.

Nevertheless, her half-brother must sing, she thought. It did not matter to her whether he should sing the wrong song or another one. All she needed him to do was to sing.

She kept singing the song of hope, and a tone of sadness and fear replaced her assertiveness. Then, like a lost cub that could not scare a furious hissing cat, her directive tone was replaced by a crying one that begged NooaKhi instead. Her panicked head bounced between the horizon, the moon, and NooaKhi's face, waiting for him to respond to her song. KaiKa then walked to her half-brother, held his hair from the back, and started to raise her voice at him. But, with every phrase of her song, NooaKhi kept pulling his head away from her grip, sliding her body towards his in the process. Finally, KaiKa adjusted and stood up on her toes. She reached up to both his ears and pulled them down with all her power. She bent NooaKhi's entire body to the back from head to toe. He screamed in pain. KaiKa released his ear, instantly regretting the mistake she had made and the errors caused by her temperament. NooaKhi turned to face KaiKa, then pushed the tribe leader's face with all his force into the ground. He pressed her head deep enough for the sand to fill her ears. He released KaiKa right before she wiped off her shock and randomly kicked the air. Untouched by her kicking, NooaKhi ran around the big rock wanting to be left alone.

NooaKhi was at peace with the thought of not fathering any of SeeKa's children. He could not accept KaiKa's allowance of child-bearing at a time when Sand was hiding around. He could not accept KaiKa's madness and the wrong songs she sang. NooaKhi had tolerated the low rankings that KaiKa often announced. He had tolerated the unjust distribution of the food he hunted with his own hands. He had endured the continuous humiliation of his hating sister. He had suppressed the fire that was burning inside him. No one has rubbed hands since KaiKa's mother's death. Now the rub of the islanders' hands grew the flames of the fire he worked so hard to keep small and unnoticed. NooaKhi was frustrated for not possessing the power of song that could have crowned him as the strong tribe chief he wanted to be. He was angry about his own body. He was mad that his voice was as ugly as his penis. He was mad that the mice he caught would always end in someone else's stomach. He was furious that he did not earn his tribe's trust, respect, or fear. He was angry that neither LaKhi nor SeeKa ever offered any comfort or alliance against KaiKa. His temper would not allow him to fake calmness and did not allow him to sing a single note from KaiKa's song of hope.

KaiKa stood up and followed him. She was determined to put an end to his blasphemous silence. She thought that his rejection of the song of hope would call the sandstorms and tornadoes and punish them all. She believed that he was offending Sand with his resentful silence and could cause rage that might put them all under siege for a hundred nights.

LaKhi and SeeKa were far down in the darkness of the caves and away from the battle that sparked between the two older islanders. They eagerly held each other's hands and clambered down into their favourite spot in the cave. When LaKhi and SeeKa reached their place, the two stopped singing and immediately started making love.

She knew every bit and piece of his body and face already. The darkness did not stop her from seeing his face. His acne scars on his thin cheeks, his tiny lips popping out of his big wild beard, his thick unruly hair, his crooked nostrils and eyes, and the three deep creases that crossed the scars he had on his forehead. She played a lot with his stiff muscles, small bitten earlobes, and rough palms. She knew what to do, where to go, and how to please him. She has been both avoiding and waiting for this moment for so long. She feared the pain of a growing womb. She feared the possibility of losing a child or her own life for Sand. But also, to love LaKhi, and to grow into becoming a mother was her only path towards wealth and status. As a mother, she would always rank second. She might even become the one and only mother. That could, one day, transform her into a queen. That could also transform KaiKa into a loyal serving priest. She thought of all the food offered to her and her children.

While dreaming of her tiny kingdom of sand. SeeKa laid down on her back over a rock, cleansed her fear, and allowed LaKhi to be on top and inside her body. She held his head and led his body in and out.

In the past, LaKhi had touched SeeKa's thighs and buttocks, the back of her neck, and touched her breast many times before and witnessed her responses to him. He never slipped inside her, though. LaKhi was yet to discover how she responded to him inside her as if he was scouting an entirely new island for the very first time.

SeeKa opened her mouth to sing, but her song squealed and became air. LaKhi had bitten her shoulder. Instantly, she bit his head in return. Now, hurt by the mutual bites, the two lovers released each other. He held both her arms, pushed her against the rock, and picked up his pace inside of her while she bit her lips. LaKhi poured himself inside her body. She received his fluids three times, and in between their two acts, they kissed and cuddled. They were not planning to stop. Every time he released his liquids, LaKhi thought of the number of children he would have from SeeKa. Four. Six. Ten. An army that would fight for the life of their queen.

They were still going for their fourth act before they were interrupted by the loud shouts of terror KaiKa, NooaKhi, and AiYi sent down into the cave's throat. The three islanders rushed into the cave and started to block the entrance with rocks.

A sandstorm had erupted out of nowhere. It dampened the dome of the night and then blocked the stars and the moon from watching what might happen to the islanders. It crawled into the island unannounced with no roars or barks. With a thousand leers on its thousand faces, the sandstorm trapped the five islanders in their caverns once again.

After scaling the entrance with rocks, AiYi led KaiKa and NooaKhi into the cave's depths to join LaKhi and SeeKa. The two lovers were irritated because of the interruption to their lovemaking but instantly anxious and troubled by KaiKa's and AiYi's song of fear.

They were all troubled by KaiKa's delusive judgment.

* * *

Trapped inside their caves, all tribe members, except for NooaKhi, gathered around KaiKa and sang their song of fear.

LaKhi and SeeKa were feeling safer than usual. They now had each other, with their arms wrapping their bodies, forming a solid alliance against starvation and death. Also, there had been no sandstorms or tornadoes for a while, and they had had several rewarding hunting nights. There was enough food to last a long time.

It was the norm for a chief to lead the tribe through the song of fear with a brave voice that lifted their spirits and reminded them to remain calm, strong, courageous, focused, sane, unified, and resilient. But the islanders sensed that KaiKa's voice was fragile and ruptured, and her song of fear was oddly sorrowful and mournful. It was not the song they expected to hear on the first day of a sandstorm. Nor was it a song they would expect to attend immediately after a song of hope. The islanders were shattered. They were trying to read KaiKa's voice, while KaiKa's mind, body, and voice struggled to put together her courage and confidence into a song.

KaiKa stopped her song. They all stopped. KaiKa wanted to clear her mind; scout the endless darkness for a single thought. She was terrified. She searched her mind with an awful limp. She had carried boulders of confidence, but they were now falling off her hands. She could not read anything.

She went back to every pebble and grain she registered while sand-reading earlier that day. She thought of all the faces and songs LaKhi, SeeKa, and NooaKhi made during the past days and nights. She went back again and thought of AiYi's face in the morning. KaiKa thought of how sure she was of what she had read. But then NooaKhi proved her wrong. She thought that she had read enough harmony and love among all islanders. Still, she could not resist blaming it all on NooaKhi. She counted his foolishness, recklessness, hatred, and anger as reasons why he insisted that she was wrong. His pride was mighty enough for him to refuse the song of hope, she thought. NooaKhi was now recklessly rejecting the song of fear, too. It must be jealousy, KaiKa thought. It must be that NooaKhi was jealous of LaKhi's voice, the second rank, and the permission to be a father to SeeKa's children. KaiKa was convinced that NooaKhi's rebellious silence was just his reaction to being left out of SeeKa and LaKhi's love.

KaiKa was taught that once an islander refused to sing, life as they knew it would change forever.

Sand tricked her, she thought. Sand was testing them. Sand fooled her into thinking it was time for hope, only to reveal that her tribe was not in harmony enough to be hopeful. She had been deceived. She thought of how her mother would have never fallen to Sand's trickery the way she had fallen. KaiKa was drowning in shame.

Meanwhile, AiYi again felt the presence of the phantom she saw while sand-reading on the beach.

Chapter Three
Songs of Mercy and Fury

Time had passed, and the cavern's residents could not tell anymore whether it was the sun or the moon that sat at the centre of the sky above their massive rock. Hunger had now replaced their sun, and thirst their moon, and both hunger and thirst were not as accurate as their sky was. Hunger and thirst did not take turns like the moon and the sun. Thirst met hunger more than the moon had ever met the sun. LaKhi wished he could make a hole at the cave's entrance to peek and see the colour of the sandstorm. He wanted to see the world around them. Was the sandstorm brown and dimming the sun, or was it black and hiding the moon? LaKhi would not dare, though. KaiKa would not allow it.

In the deepest rooms of the cave, the rocks were cold and moist. And in the upper levels of the cave, islanders could feel the heat blowing in through the pores of the cave's entrance. They felt the dryness of the walls. The heat and dry walls were two vital signs an islander would look for to check if the sandstorm was still raging outside.

AiYi and LaKhi would check the airflow from the pores found in the buried cave's entrance. Like a mother examining a child's throat for airflow to check if the child was alive; AiYi and LaKhi, on the contrary, were hoping for the absence of air.

A mouse or a snake sneaking through the cracks was a third vital sign. An intruding animal brought both joy and anguish to the islanders' hearts. It was fresh meat, yet, a reminder that the sandstorm was still hungry and after them, like an insomniac hunter waiting for its prey to leave its burrow.

AiYi would patrol the upper floors of the cave and touch every wall and ceiling, looking for dew or tiny streams of water droplets seeping through the cracks. She looked for any sign of sandstorms being rinsed off the surface of the roofs of the two large rocky beds that sit at the island's heart. She sniffed and hoped to find any trace and smell of mud.

The islanders' pile of cured sand mice meat and the little pond of cold water continued to tame their bad-tempered bodies. KaiKa's songs of hunger and thirst were sung with her back rested on the cavern walls, so her voice could travel deep inside. Her songs continued to tame their minds and protect them all from the dark hallucinations and ghosts that haunted them in silence. Her songs also made their restless minds fall asleep.

For these islanders, dreams were a great escape from their dark reality. They were liberating. SeeKa often dreamt of the ocean. LaKhi, on the other hand, had many dreams of him walking on the sand out in the open. He just saw his feet walk. SeeKa, LaKhi, and AiYi always appeared in KaiKa and NooaKhi's dreams. AiYi was unaware that all other four islanders enjoyed illusions of freedom now and then.

LaKhi and SeeKa kept close to each other. Always tied together. His hands were locked in her hands. Her legs between his legs. And when she slept, he always kept awake for a while, listening to her breathe.

NooaKhi isolated himself in a corner behind the water pond. He spent most of his time in silence, assembling and disassembling lines and piles of pebbles and frequently yawning or snoring in the dark.

In the timeless darkness, their sleep was all of a sudden disturbed by SeeKa ceaselessly coughing and moaning. She was struggling in the dark trying to grasp a breath. KaiKa rushed towards her. It must have been NooaKhi, she thought. His hatred and vengeance only erupted in the darkness. Her heart pounded. She imagined his hands wrapped around SeeKa's neck. AiYi raced KaiKa and reached SeeKa first. They both felt LaKhi present and sitting next to SeeKa, while she emptied her stomach. KaiKa stepped over SeeKa's spew, and AiYi smelled it. SeeKa was still coughing and trying to catch a breath. They touched SeeKa's body and felt a blanket of sweat, her mouth and nose drooling. KaiKa ran to the water pond in the dark and filled her hands with water. She dropped most of it on her way back to SeeKa but managed to carry enough water to moisten SeeKa's throat. Both LaKhi and AiYi did the same and came back with more water.

Gradually, SeeKa stopped sweating and breathed regularly. KaiKa carefully reached out to SeeKa and slid two of her fingers into her sister's vagina. Then KaiKa, like an unpractised juvenile canine, brought her fingers close to her nose and took several long sniffs. She was looking for the fresh smell of a new soul inside her sister's body. She then tasted her fingers. Still unsure, KaiKa took another swipe and tasted her fingers again. She analysed and smelled her finger again. Then, KaiKa leaned toward SeeKa's breasts and touched her nipples, then pinched each one of them. KaiKa felt them again and again. They were hardened, dry, and more pronounced than usual. Finally, KaiKa lifted SeeKa's breasts and slapped them up several times as if she were weighing each looking for mass and stiffness that did not exist before. LaKhi and SeeKa sensed that KaiKa was performing the ancient mothers' routine they had both witnessed being performed on KaiKa by her mother. LaKhi's nerves were trembling. His feet and hands were restless. He waited for an important announcement.

KaiKa smiled. She took two more oozy swipes, and lifted her finger close to SeeKa's face before wiping one finger on SeeKa's cheeks. SeeKa's squicked lips transformed into the largest smile she had had for a while. KaiKa then tapped her second finger over LaKhi's forehead. She then took a deep breath, rubbed her palms, and sang the song of hope with laughter and extreme joy. KaiKa was dancing. LaKhi instantly clapped and jumped in excitement and began to sing with KaiKa. AiYi was confused and waiting for an explanation. But despite her puzzled state of mind, AiYi instantly joined the two and started to rub her hands and sing. KaiKa held AiYi's hands, and they danced together.

When the dancing ceased, KaiKa returned to SeeKa and laid her left hand over her sister's belly button and her right over her head and sang in a joyful, comforting voice. SeeKa quickly realized that this was her motherhood ceremony— KaiKa's hands like the crown worn by mothers over her head and the baby held in her belly like an ancient magical sceptre. SeeKa responded in laughter and echoed KaiKa's song. She accepted her motherly crown and maternal duties. She received the high ranks and all the goods that came with it. She took her inheritance and all that was once possessed by the mothers. The water, food, attention and care, respect, and her new worth. SeeKa's life was now the most critical among her tribe members. She was sitting on a bright throne only made visible to SeeKa, KaiKa, and the mothers of Sand Island. If only LaKhi and NooaKhi could see my crown, SeeKa thought. Instead, LaKhi and KaiKa could only sense the massive smile on SeeKa's face.

Through her song of hope, KaiKa announced that SeeKa was indeed fruitful and carrying a child in her womb. She revealed the presence of a mother among them. She sang the song of hope with joy and triumph and danced as if she had won a battle, dedicating her victory to all the mothers she once knew. NooaKhi stood silently at a distance but listened carefully.

But KaiKa was also hiding the song of fear that played in her mind. She hid the tremendous danger she sensed coming ahead. Like KaiKa, who had lost her three unborn children to Sand and in sandstorms, most mothers on Sand Island lost their unborn children while being trapped inside their caves. Some were fortunate to eat their flesh; others, unfortunately, had to drop their unborn babies as loot for Sand as they ran for their lives away from evil Sand monsters. And like

LaKhi's mother, who lost her life after giving birth to him inside the caves during a sandstorm, many others died during labour or a few nights after giving birth. They died inside the caves, soaked in pools of blood.

As much as they were singing and dancing festively and were happy about SeeKa's pregnancy, KaiKa, and the vigilant LaKhi, were also worried that the birth of a child could harm SeeKa. She was the last fertile woman. So at once, SeeKa's health became the most precious currency on Sand Island.

KaiKa believed that all the sacrifices her mother had ever made, and the sacrifices made by every mother that had ever lived on Sand Islands, all led to SeeKa bringing yet again the miracle of life into this lifeless island. Therefore, KaiKa now carried the most important tasks ever given to any leader that had ever lived on this island; KaiKa must keep SeeKa alive till she gave birth to her child. She must keep SeeKa alive to breastfeed and wean her child. And she must keep SeeKa alive till she gave birth to another child, and another, and another.

Soon to be a father, LaKhi, surrounded SeeKa all day long, keeping her body bathed, warm, and protected from Sand. He must protect her from hunger and thirst, twin evils of the cave's darkness. He must also defend her from NooaKhi, the dangerous islander who had stopped singing. Meanwhile, the soon-to-be midwife, KaiKa, shared cured sand mice meat from her stash with SeeKa. KaiKa knew that SeeKa would need regular and adequate portions of food so she and her baby could overcome this sandstorm.

SeeKa enjoyed the special treatment from LaKhi and KaiKa and was now seeking the same from little blind AiYi who remained clueless about these irregular festivities in the dark. KaiKa could not explain to AiYi the cause of the delight. She did not bother to unlock AiYi's generosity in favour of an upcoming mother and child.

Although LaKhi and SeeKa did not witness the fights between NooaKhi and KaiKa, they still felt the battle. They were irritated by his stubbornness and his protest against all

the songs KaiKa sang. No mad father they knew had dared
to remain silent during a song. NooaKhi's silence introduced
new mischievous practices they had not known before. His
silence was extremely violent. With every song, LaKhi felt
sad; his beloved brother was silently turning mad. With every
song, SeeKa felt disgusted; NooaKhi was disrespecting the
will of mothers. But LaKhi and SeeKa both thought that
NooaKhi was already doing them all a favour by keeping
his distance from SeeKa's nest. Keeping them all unbothered.

It was only after several water-drinking ceremonies that
AiYi sensed that SeeKa was with child. The two additional
long sips that SeeKa was granted had become a new norm.
AiYi realized that they were all in the presence of a new soul.
SeeKa held AiYi's hand and led AiYi's hand to her belly. The
little blind girl giggled, her chest filled with wonder and joy.
AiYi even offered her own mice meat to SeeKa. And the
very hungry SeeKa gladly accepted AiYi's offerings without
any hesitations or remorse.

NooaKhi sensed the gifts AiYi made in the dark. Ashamed
of himself, he walked over to SeeKa carrying an offering
of two pieces of cured mice meat. He accidentally held
her arm in the dark. SeeKa must have felt alarmed at his
grip and instinctively slapped NooaKhi's hand and pushed
him away, screaming like a siren. LaKhi, KaiKa, and AiYi
woke up to SeeKa's shriek. LaKhi jumped towards them,
pushing NooaKhi's body away and blocking him from
SeeKa. NooaKhi pushed his half-brother's face in the dark
and sauntered back to his lair, sickened by their rejection of
his gifts. He was hurt by the hate KaiKa had seeded in their
hearts for him. KaiKa touched her half-sister's face and held
her arms to calm her down.

AiYi went back to sleep when all the noise and heavy
breathing faded. LaKhi and SeeKa, however, did not sleep
for long after their confrontation with NooaKhi. Joined by
KaiKa, all three had their eyes wide open in the dark, steering
their ears for any signs of movement and sniffing the air for
changes in scent.

* * *

Meanwhile, the sandstorm continued to rage outside. The island was scraping its skin, like a mad primate, struggling with a poisonous rash. Sand scouted the surface of the island for bones and rocks to chew. Anxiety and panic filled the darkness in the cave, like a thick, black tar pouring down their heads. Whispers of the song of fear dominated the cavern's small chambers and narrow halls like an army of termites eating the ins and outs of a hundred-year-old tree.

When KaiKa had been pregnant, she did not tolerate NooaKhi's snoring whenever he slept close to her. She would kick him away and humiliated him in front of the other mothers and fathers who laughed at him. Welcome to fatherhood, they all joked. Now every time KaiKa sang, she wished she would hear NooaKhi snoring. She would take more comfort in knowing that he was asleep than in the discomfort caused by his silence.

KaiKa sauntered in the darkness to where she expected to find NooaKhi lying down. Instead, her body bumped into another that seemed like the depth of the cave's darkness. She had bumped into her half-brother's body. He was there, standing and breathing heavily, looking right into the deep dark silhouette of her face. KaiKa felt his breath swiftly brush her large forehead.

KaiKa raised her hand to touch NooaKhi's face, then reached into his mouth. Eight of her fingertips were begging him. Her fingers bowed to his face for forgiveness and mercy. She then held NooaKhi's lips, moved his mouth, and sang the song of hope on his behalf, asking him to join her song. NooaKhi growled, then slapped his half-sister's hand and pulled himself away from her, into the darkness and towards his quiet corner.

KaiKa could not bear the weight of her brother's anger and envy. She sat down and sang the song of hope, filling her voice with her tears until she could no longer carry their weight on her voice and face. Finally, she stopped singing and sobbed like an injured animal. Every cry travelled into the cave's halls and pores like the blood that spanned the body through the veins. Echoes of KaiKa's screams filled the void between a moan and another. The other three islanders heard her cries, and KaiKa's image grew older and weaker with every scream. Her strength and power were like a giant sculpture, built out of lumber, burning slowly and turning into ashes and vanishing in the air.

AiYi crawled in the dark towards KaiKa's cries. She found KaiKa lying down sobbing with her eyes fastened to the ground through a stream of tears. AiYi touched KaiKa's head. Realizing how much of a right and a privilege it was for her to touch KaiKa's head—and how rarely had done it in the past—the little girl leaned in towards KaiKa wanting to hug her head. But KaiKa got irritated. She swatted away AiYi's hand and kicked her with her knees. The little blind girl fell off her crouch but did not move far. She did not cry, or even make a sound. She simply sat next to KaiKa, pulling her legs into her chest and listening to KaiKa crying until KaiKa fell asleep.

* * *

LaKhi and NooaKhi were invisible to each other and avoided each other since SeeKa's rejection of NooaKhi's mouse meat. In all previous sandstorms, the two half-brothers would barter meat and even put their mice meat into a joint food inventory. At times like these, LaKhi always shared back the food NooaKhi hunted with his elder brother. NooaKhi always made sure LaKhi got most of the food LaKhi shared. Though NooaKhi was always outranked by his younger brother, LaKhi always treated NooaKhi as the outranking brother. They would spend time playing games in the dark. They would guess in which hand the other had hidden a pebble. Or, guess how many fingers the other had folded and shared answers by touching each other's hands. They aimed and threw small pebbles at each other in the dark. Whoever got hit the most won. They would even fool each other by not shouting in pain whenever hit by a pebble. A burst of laughter by LaKhi sometimes would reveal that he had been hit many times but was cheating by keeping his defeat unannounced.

This sandstorm was the first that had them stay apart. The two half-brothers did not barter. Did not play. And did not laugh or touch. They wanted to approach each other and missed the other. But in reality, they pretended as if they were trapped in separate caves.

KaiKa was now sure that she had misread Sand. She did not give up, though. Instead, she spent more time close to the cave's entrance with LaKhi and AiYi. She heard the Sand's ghastly aeolian whispers and whistles. She carefully read Sand. And she read that Sand had demands. She believed that Sand had conditions too. She read that sandstorms were only there to trap NooaKhi. She thought that Sand was bargaining for their salvation. Sand was willing to offer their freedom in exchange for NooaKhi's song of hope or his death. In all this, the thought that kept KaiKa most vigil and anxious was the burden of keeping all the islanders alive. She must keep singing. She must guide NooaKhi to adulthood through song. She shook off the idea of sacrifice.

KaiKa must force NooaKhi to end this sandstorm by joining their song of hope. She could not consider offering her half-brother as a sacrifice, yet. Any attempt to kill NooaKhi could lead to bloodshed. NooaKhi was no sand mouse. He would not give up his life easily. He was as fierce as a tornado. He had arms that could pick up any islander's body and pierce it through the cave's spiny walls and roofs. She was confident that there would be collateral damage if she made any attempt of offering her brother to Sand. She knew that she would end up offering more than a half-brother.

* * *

KaiKa silently sneaked into NooaKhi's bed. She crawled on the ground next to him and poked his face. NooaKhi woke up annoyed and sighed at his sister, but also showed her some respect by sitting up straight in a partly welcoming position. It was as if he were waiting for her to ask for something.

KaiKa touched his knee and let her hand rest there. He touched her lips. While he was asking her to remain silent, KaiKa thought he was inviting her to sing. She smiled softly in the dark and started to hum the song of hope. She calmly invited him to join her, hoping that he would overcome his defiance and start acting selflessly in the interest of the tribe. However, NooaKhi was behaving like a mute who had no choice but to remain silent. KaiKa's smile now vanished. Tears pricked her eyes. She kept singing the song of hope, while NooaKhi remained silent.

Though KaiKa believed that Sand demanded a song of hope, her song's tone, with perfection, shifted from the song of hope to the most melancholic song the tribe had ever experienced—the song of mercy. A song that was reserved to only be sung to Sand. A song that was only sung by a tribe leader to an islander at times of defeat and surrender. A song that always led to drastic paths no matter what the direction was. It was the last reserve that expressed the most profound depth of desperation. It was only sung in tears, the purest instrument one could use in a song and the most challenging instrument to play. The song of mercy could easily slip and produce dissonance if tears were not handled with utmost delicacy. KaiKa gave her title and crown to her half-brother with her song of mercy. A sacrifice that would keep her tribe alive, she believed. KaiKa thought she could come back to the song of hope, the song Sand demanded, once she begged her way to NooaKhi's softened heart.

NooaKhi reached out to her face and pressed his finger to her lips. Now that she had handed over her crown, his first command was for KaiKa to be quiet. But she did not respond to his command. Annoyed by how well KaiKa played her tears and song, NooaKhi stood up. He was about to leave his space. Still, KaiKa tightened her hands onto NooaKhi's legs while moaning and singing the song of mercy, now in dissonance.

A heavy fluid shadow flooded the pores of the cave and was filling its rooms with sorrow and uncertainty. While NooaKhi dragged his feet in the dark with his half-sister clutching onto them, the other three islanders stood up in their places silently listening to KaiKa crying like never before and terrified by the weakness they never thought she had.

NooaKhi walked down the steps leading to the cave's largest pond, and KaiKa's rough skin was further torn by the sharp rocks beneath her ragged body. The pain was unbearable for KaiKa. She had to unlock her grip, kneel, then clear her throat and fill her lungs with one big breath before she wept aloud, the saddest song she ever sang. Her song sent a wave of echoes across the cave's rooms and walls that breached the pores of the cave, travelled against the sandstorms, and reached the ocean for the sea to roar back at it. KaiKa's song sent sharp chills through AiYi and SeeKa, breaking their silence, and shocking LaKhi into an unprecedented state of paralysis.

When the echoes of the last stanza of KaiKa's song of mercy faded, the islanders could hear NooaKhi's cries and sniffles. They could hear him weep in sadness and anger.

KaiKa took NooaKhi's tears as an opportunity. She ran towards the sound of his sniffles and hugged him. Both cried together for a few moments wrapped in each other's arms. Then, when KaiKa felt her half-brother softening in her arms, she started to sing the song of hope again.

NooaKhi placed his palm over her mouth, requesting her to stop singing for the third time. She proudly declined his request, yet again. KaiKa's voice was now shouting out in anger the song of hope. Her hands shook as they reached his neck. One hand pressed his beard against his chin while the other wrapped itself around the back of his neck.

NooaKhi instantly rolled his arms around his half-sister in a hug. She felt progress. Her eyes shifted in joy, and her tears were transforming. Her nose was running, and a happy giggle escaped her throat.

But NooaKhi tightened his arms around her. His muscles were hardened and his veins thickened. His terrified eyes were wide open, staring into the dark, ready to pop out of his skull. KaiKa's song and voice started to fade in pain. She knew that she was in extreme danger. Her voice had vanished. The other three islanders approached the sounds of NooaKhi and KaiKa's struggling footsteps.

NooaKhi powerfully carried KaiKa off the ground and swung his body around to throw KaiKa in the direction of the primary drinking water pond. Just before he flung her body in the air, KaiKa managed to make a faint sound that carried the intensity of her pain. Then, there was a big splash. The other islanders moved closer to the scene, wanting to apprehend what was happening. The aggression was silent yet felt through the darkness like a stampede. The despair was so loud before it plunged into the depth of the water pond. NooaKhi stepped into the pond and towards the splash KaiKa's body had made.

AiYi and SeeKa moved closer to the troubling foreign noise from beneath the surface of the water. It was KaiKa struggling to breathe. NooaKhi was sitting over KaiKa's back with his legs extended over her shoulder. In this position, KaiKa's head was pressed against the floor of the pond. NooaKhi had leaned over her head with his elbows pressing down her broken skull.

When the islanders realized that they were about to lose their chief to death, AiYi and SeeKa exploded into an outraged song. It was the angriest song ever sung on Sand Island, the song of fury. The only song that allowed islanders to take their voices to the promontories of madness. The loudest sounds a throat could make, the most potent blows and howls a lung could produce. With mouths and eyes wide open facing the cave's ceilings, SeeKa and AiYi blew four and five sequences before they stopped to check if that inscrutable sound of water had calmed down or was still raging. LaKhi remained shocked in silence.

The three islanders could now only hear NooaKhi breathing quickly and heavily.

AiYi moved closer to where NooaKhi was. She stepped over KaiKa's feet. KaiKa did not mind being stepped over. AiYi did not get the slap she had hoped she would get from her loving chief. AiYi lifted KaiKa's leg and held onto it only to realize that she was no longer carrying the living leg of her beloved singing chief. It was now a part of a damaged corpse.

Sand had crawled into the cave and possessed NooaKhi's body. That is what LaKhi believed. NooaKhi's body was only obeying Sand's commands.

AiYi turned her head towards NooaKhi, who was still breathing heavily, and fell on her knees while howling again, a softer and broken song of fury. She sang her song in protest of NooaKhi's fratricide and anarchy.

NooaKhi at once waded towards AiYi splashing the water angrily. After tracing where her head was, he covered her mouth. AiYi bit NooaKhi's hand, and he slapped AiYi's face so hard her bruise shocked all the tears off her cheeks. He kept slapping her face. By the eighth slap, AiYi could no longer bite NooaKhi's hand any harder and released his hand. Finally, NooaKhi pushed AiYi's face, but not hard enough to knock her down on the ground. He moved out of the pond and back to his den.

SeeKa snapped out of her shock when she heard NooaKhi's footsteps fading away and blew another howl of her song of fury in protest. However, this time, LaKhi ran towards SeeKa, and from behind her back, he covered her mouth, signalling her to stop the song. He instructed her to accept NooaKhi's demands and reign.

For the rest of the night, the cave walls could not help but keep echoing the weeping sounds made by AiYi, SeeKa, and LaKhi.

NooaKhi's tears were as quiet as the surface of the pond's water.

For the first time in their lives, the four islanders were silent.

* * *

Without hesitation or an official announcement, singing was forbidden by the new unannounced self-proclaimed chief, NooaKhi. No one shall sing ever again. Remain silent or die. That was the first amendment in Sand Island laws and the only law dictated by NooaKhi.

SeeKa was threatened once by NooaKhi and protected by LaKhi when she attempted to initiate the song of hunger while eating her first meal after KaiKa's death.

AiYi got slapped by NooaKhi twice because she attempted to sing her favourite song, the song of thirst. Her attempt was not only an attempt to pay respect to Sand but also to appease her anger and pain from the loss she had. For she had lost another mother.

LaKhi did not bother to sing any songs. It was as if the only thing he could see in the total darkness of the cave was NooaKhi's new rule against singing and his anger.

Chapter Four
Silence

Time and its workings were not common knowledge on Sand Island.

Time was mainly present.

A little bit of time could fit as future, and even less of it was shelved as past. And all of time was merely a pathetic servant to Sand.

The future was dull. Easy to predict. Always full of sand.

The past instantly faded. As if it never existed.

Memories were past's only saviour. To remember and tell stories, then retell what one remembered, was the only trail one could follow to be unforgotten. With no stories to tell or remember on Sand Island, everything and everyone was instantly forgotten.

Dreams were nightmares of the past. To witness what was real, alone or together, and dream of self or others, was all equal. Dreams and realities all faded if they could not be passed from one islander to another. If one cannot tell what was real or what was ideal, and what had happened or not, the past, instantly faded as if it never existed.

Emotions from the past piled up. Emotions were carried. Heavy or light, they were carried into the present, without sight of how time was there, day and night.

The sun was a disciplined peasant; it rose and set every day on Sand Island. The sun was a futile merchant; it bartered

day for night, and night for day. It was an awful poet; it failed
to make meanings of night and day on Sand Island.

* * *

Five days had passed since KaiKa's death.

The islanders were still in shock. Except for SeeKa, they
did not eat or move away from their weeping spots. They did
not touch or comfort each other as if they were all terrified of
each other. They were afraid of NooaKhi and also afraid of
their inability to protect KaiKa from a murderer. They were
all threatened by NooaKhi and themselves.

Each had a few sips of water. No one sought anyone's
permission to drink water. They drank their water in no
particular order. They just did what they had to do to keep
their guts wet and their bodies alive.

Those five days felt like anything between five moments to
five weeks. It was not uncommon for trapped islanders to lose
track of day and night when under the siege of Sand. They
had experienced harsh sandstorms that lasted long enough to
make them feel as if life and time had stopped entirely.

Sandstorms and tornadoes kept islanders away from the
cosmic phenomenon of day and night. Thus, Sand was capable
of stopping time. However, with Sand songs, islanders had
the privilege of logging their activities and emotions. With
their songs, they transformed time from its universal form
that moved their island against the sun into a non-universal
state that disregarded the moon and its position in the sky.
Through Sand songs, islanders were able to smuggle time
from its universal borders and transform it into something
fluid that they could play with and pass over to each other
in the dark.

Sand songs were their reference to what they did and how
they felt in total darkness. It was the norm to stop counting
days and nights while trapped in the cave's darkness. But it
was also the norm to replace their days, nights, and moments
with the songs they counted. Trapped islanders would count

two songs of hunger and then sleep. They registered facts. They noted that they slept after two songs of hunger, and their sleep was followed by a song of thirst. They remembered that they played after a single song of thirst and remembered that they kissed after a couple of songs of fear.

Each carried a memory of their own. Each had a register of their own. So, each islander's sense of time varied from another. A fortunate islander would carry time that moved fast enough to make a sandstorm last for what might be a couple of nights. For a depressed islander, the same might be different, denser, one that moved slowly to make the same sandstorm last for what seemed to be a hundred nights.

Sand songs moved time adequately enough in the darkness until songs stopped Sand from its madness. And once sandstorms stopped, the sun and the moon slid into their world. The universal form of time moved again on Sand Island.

Sand stopped time in their caves.

Songs bent time in the dark and moved it.

And time was relevant in the dark; time moved faster or slower depending on how much time an islander was capable of lifting.

Those were the laws of time the islanders have almost known.

In the past five days in total darkness and silence, there were no Sand songs to count. Time had stopped. And they could not bend it anymore. Nor was it relevant anymore. So the laws of time on Sand Island were amended into a new single law—Sand and silence stopped and paralysed time completely in the dark.

The silence did not give the islanders the same power they once had to transform time into something they could control. Time was entirely absent. They could not slow it. They could not make it gallop. They could not navigate through it. They could not see it. Like an infinite maze with no entrances or exits, islanders were lost in time. And the songs they once sang, the map they once held, were lit into a fire and changed to flying ashes that blended into the sandstorm.

In silence, islanders stepped into a parallel island. Their world seemed like they were living in a parallel universe. It was still them, and it was still the cave they knew. It was still the darkness they called home. And still, the Sand they always feared. Yet it was no longer the world they all once knew.

AiYi, SeeKa, and LaKhi were completely lost. They missed KaiKa. She would have sung many songs that could have indicated five days since her death. Her body did not sing. Time ceased to exist in KaiKa's silence. The sun ceased to exist beyond the walls of their caves.

* * *

The four islanders woke up to a feeling of wetness. Water was soaking their bodies wet. It was oddly rising inside the cave. None of them was sure how and where all the water had come from. This was a new phenomenon they had never dealt with before—one they could not study, explain, or discuss.

A tiny amount of moisture and dew was all they needed to know that a sandstorm or a tornado had abandoned the island. A small amount of flooding water that could not drown them was benign and did not threaten them; yet, it was novel enough to send absolute terror and chills to their soaked skins and sinking ankles.

Confused and highly anxious, NooaKhi and LaKhi dashed to the cave entrance to dig themselves out of it. SeeKa and AiYi stood right behind them, shivering in terror. Then, finally, the two men found an opening. NooaKhi forced himself out and pushed the rocks away in every direction using his shoulders and head. NooaKhi sprinted out of the cave, running as far as possible from the entrance. LaKhi went back, held SeeKa and AiYi's hands, and followed NooaKhi out of the cave and into the open.

NooaKhi, followed by the other three islanders, stood in front of the cave entrance, looking up in awe at the rain.

They looked at a large dark weeping cloud that blocked the sun and touched the peaks of their rocky mountains. AiYi did not look up. Instead, she walked on her toes in circles, fleeing away from the water and the mud beneath her feet. She could not find a single spot that was recognizably dry.

The four islanders had never witnessed or experienced rain while outside the cave. They did not know of it or how it looked. None of their mothers or fathers had ever prepared them for such an event. Clouds had always made brief visits that rinsed sandstorms, but the islanders were usually late in emerging from their caves so had never actually seen a rain-bearing cloud. All the clouds they ever sensed were too shy to confront the islanders. This cloud was daringly confrontational. This cloud was arrogantly parading and carefree. It had no regard for Sand and its monsters.

NooaKhi, LaKhi, and SeeKa stood there for long, startled. Then they started to look at each other, then looked up again, mesmerized by the cloud's shape.

SeeKa wanted to initiate a song but had no idea which song to sing. There was so much water. At first she thought of the song of thirst. But the clouds and rain were all new and terrifying. So, it could also be the song of fear, or another unknown song that only KaiKa and the mothers could have sung. Only if KaiKa were alive, she would have guided them on how to react to rain and clouds, LaKhi thought.

SeeKa was now on her way to become a mother, and KaiKa was no more than a body that would be soon buried in the dunes or eaten by the ocean. She wanted to practice sand-reading and better understand what to do and how like every mother, she ever knew. That's what mothers do, she thought. She had a higher appetite for festivities and excitement. She was tired of being afraid. SeeKa, suddenly, broke her silence and started to sing the song of thirst. Her very first tone sent out a signal of comfort to AiYi, who felt lost under the rain. Just as AiYi was about to open her mouth and sing, NooaKhi jumped at SeeKa and covered her mouth with his two hands. Within a moment, LaKhi jumped in, adding a third hand over NooaKhi's two. Neither man was aggressive in their grip. They were just gently co-leading SeeKa into silence again. They both feared that SeeKa would scare the cloud away.

The sky poured all day. Finally, the two men dragged KaiKa's body out of the cave while SeeKa held AiYi's hands and walked around the cave to comfort the little girl.

KaiKa's body was taken out of the cave and left in the open under the rain and close to her favourite sand-reading spot, not far from where her mother's body was left to rest before Sand carried her out of their sight. SeeKa led AiYi to KaiKa's body to let her know she rested.

Though the norm was to feast on a dead islander's body, the young islanders were too weak, like a frail vulture unable to fly, to rush into that kind of a sombre meal. So, instead, they ate leftover cured mice from their last hunt. They opened their mouths and were served water by the gentle cloud. They found different spots around their caves where the water trickled through the rocks. They drank as much clean, freshwater as they pleased.

NooaKhi took a stroll out in the open. This time, LaKhi asked for NooaKhi's permission to walk with him. NooaKhi did not mind. The two young men went far away from the cave, still under the shade of the big raining cloud. They went far and beyond the area where they used to hunt. NooaKhi then raced his brother back to the cave's entrance. They were playing again. The two brothers laid down inside the cave but close to the entrance and away from the rain. They offered their exhausted bodies a good, long sleep. SeeKa and AiYi followed the two young men, and they all gathered around each other and slept while the rain fell on the island.

* * *

The next morning, NooaKhi, SeeKa, and AiYi woke up suddenly, startled by LaKhi's voice traveling from the shore. The big raining cloud was no more. NooaKhi ran towards

LaKhi covering his eyes from the sunlight but allowing a few rays to sneak in before letting his pupils expand. SeeKa and AiYi followed cautiously, taking one step at a time.

Despite the alerts LaKhi's voice was sending, SeeKa slowed down and was distracted by the bright blue sky. The white clouds scattered across the sky were excessively more prominent than ever. It seemed like hundreds of clouds had travelled quickly and spread across the sky. They mysteriously appeared from one horizon and faded into another. The sun rays were dancing and flickering between the big white clouds. The rays touched the ground and extended the movement of the waves into the dunes and mountains. AiYi, on the other hand, was still trying to navigate her way through patches of dry sand and irregular patterns of wet sand.

NooaKhi saw LaKhi jumping up and down and around on the shore, looking into something strange that moved back and forth beneath LaKhi's legs. A bright red rock was moving and manoeuvring away from LaKhi with speed and wit. The two young men were astonished by its colour. A new colour on the island. Alive and running away from them. The bright red rock hid under a thin layer of sand. Rocks do not run and hide! LaKhi approached it while NooaKhi carefully watched. The rock had not perfectly hidden itself. A tiny bright yellow tip was still visible. Poorly performing its camouflage skills next to hungry islanders that had never seen brightly coloured moving rocks was humour that almost made the ocean splash a cough out of laughter. LaKhi poked the hard tip of the moving rock, and it ran away in the open. Bright red, on white sand under a clear blue sky.

It was a giant bright-red-shelled yellow nipper crab trying to find its way back to its newly dug burrow. NooaKhi came closer to the crab to get a better look at it. Both men circled the crab. Finally, SeeKa and AiYi arrived, and the crab fled sideways towards SeeKa, who instantly screamed several times while running away from the crab. With each scream SeeKa made, AiYi sympathetically cried in fear and confusion.

LaKhi laughed at SeeKa and ran after the crab, and NooaKhi followed, still cautious. SeeKa looked at the crab in disgust from a distance, then slowly moved towards it, curious. The two men laughed and danced around the crab, trying to catch it. SeeKa joined the dance.

AiYi heard the laughter and the footwork of all three and sensed a strange unthreatening hunt going on. She was confused since all the hunting quests she knew were nocturnal, yet there they were, trying to catch something right under the sun's warmth. Also, while hunting a mouse, there was never that amount of time to manoeuvre; a mouse would have fled into its burrow already. She sensed that they were not chasing a mouse but something rather amusing. Something new and funny. She felt that they were after an animal that came with silence. An animal that was hiding from KaiKa's songs.

The three curious islanders circled the red crab and fixed their eyes on it, carefully studying it. It was slow. It knew how to hide, but hid from their eyes poorly. They could still see it beneath a thin layer of sand. LaKhi jumped at it first. He picked it up and instantly felt scared and dropped it. NooaKhi ran after it but was not lucky or quick enough to catch it. SeeKa left the two men for a moment and came back with a rock and gave it to LaKhi, signalling him to use it to kill the crab. They all followed it, waiting for it to stop and bury itself under the sand. They anticipated it well. They were learning. The moment it hid under the sand, LaKhi threw the rock at it, and the stone cracked the crab's shell.

LaKhi picked up the crab with the tips of his nails. He touched one of the crab's spines, examining how hard and dangerous a crab could be. Then, he shook the sand off of the crab's shell and started playing with it. He tossed it over to NooaKhi, who got stung by its shell and had to drop it, then picked it up and examined the animal while LaKhi and SeeKa laughed at him. They were astonished by its pointy limbs, bright red colour, and eye-shaped shell. Then SeeKa grabbed the crab from NooaKhi's hand, carefully licked the body, and examined its taste. It was not salty nor bitter. It had an edible taste that was significantly distinguishable from the mice's meat and cacti she had eaten throughout her life. She licked one more time before she swooped in and took a bite out of its body. The spines did not bother SeeKa or stop her from chewing the giant crab's shell. She was now enjoying the crab's taste. She sucked the soft white meat. It did not taste like anything she had ever eaten before. By far it was tastier than any mice meat she ever had. Next, NooaKhi tried to pull the crab out of SeeKa's mouth and tore a claw out that he chewed. LaKhi did the same thing. The three young islanders were cracking, chewing, sucking, and spitting out crab shells. They were engrossed in a euphoric gastronomic experience they had never expected to experience. They were so occupied that they forgot to share a taste of the funny red rock with the starving little blind girl.

While the three islanders made obnoxious chewing and sucking sounds, clueless AiYi got distracted by another new sound that came from a spot far away on the beach. She moved towards the indulged SeeKa, held her arm, and pointed her finger to the source of the novel sound. The other islanders stopped chewing and raised their heads to better hear the voice AiYi was referring to. Then all four started to walk across the shoreline towards the sound. Three were still walking with pieces of crab in their hands and mouths.

A strange white animated cloud could be seen on the horizon; it was not a sandstorm or a tornado. Instead, this cloud repeatedly moved higher into the sky, then plunged and touched the ground, expanded and shrunk and swirled. It also made a lot of waggish noise that was alien to the four young islanders.

As they approached the cloud, the young islanders realized that the cloud was a large flock of birds. Looking up, they saw their clean white bellies. NooaKhi had only once heard the sound of a bird that had crawled into their caves. The bird was eaten by the fathers. He remembered the sounds it made. The cries. The few blood-stained white, black, and brown feathers the fathers could not eat. A memory only he and KaiKa had as children and kept for themselves. Seeing that many birds— and sharing that memory with the whole group—was refreshing. Something odd was happening on the island, NooaKhi thought.

As the islanders got closer to the flock, they saw hundreds of bright red crabs on the ground right below the congregation, hiding under the sand or finding their way back to their burrows or back to the sea. The flock was raiding an entire village of defenceless crabs. The birds landed on the sand, walked with their long stick-like legs, and carefully picked up tiny crabs with their shiny black beaks. These long-necked and long-feet birds with white bellies and black wings were everywhere. The island now was host to a new predator that walked on its grounds and flew over its beaches. The island's new guests were crab-eating long-necked plovers.

NooaKhi, SeeKa, and LaKhi ran towards the cast of crabs and joined forces with the congregation in an interspecies hunt festival. They were catching as many crabs as they could. NooaKhi and LaKhi followed a strategy. They captured crabs and broke their shells, then threw them aside for later. But LaKhi soon noticed that plovers were pecking and stealing their crabs from their stash, so he went after a plover, jumped at it, and broke its long legs and neck. This way they caught dozens of crabs and two plovers.

While all three were running, dancing, and jumping in ecstasy, AiYi felt lost in the absence of songs. She was lost in their silence. But also was lost in a cloud of laughter and the noise the plovers made. She felt that these creatures she heard had not come with good intentions. Animals that only appear in silence and hide from Sand songs could not come with Sand's blessings. She imagined that if KaiKa were still living among them, she would beg them to sing. She would beg them to leave those creatures alone.

AiYi, all of a sudden, felt a strange sting in her back.

AiYi turned around. Listened to the wind and whispered. 'KaiKa?'

Part II
Green Island

Chapter Five
The Song of Gratitude

The island was suspiciously changing: quickly and with no merit. A father that beat up his children to sleep and then woke them up with warm embraces and kisses, was less suspiciously transformative than the changes on the island. Sand Island had become oddly kinder to the four confused young islanders. Though they could not discuss it, they could not help but wonder why it was. The moment they had stepped out of their siege, was the moment they had stepped into an island they could no longer anticipate. Was it the silence that caused the changes? Was it KaiKa that bothered Sand? Was NooaKhi the rightful king of the island? Was Sand just teasing and playing malicious games? Or, were the clouds, crabs, and plovers just lost?

Rain drizzled softly and constantly throughout the next few full moons after KaiKa's death, keeping the island and its inhabitants pleasantly moist, alive, and growing. New freshwater ponds appeared everywhere across the island. Water overflowed and started to wash the sand and reveal ancient spring water paths. Hundreds of streams that unendingly flew outwards from the mountain tips formed small waterfalls that poured into larger ponds and streams. Water also reached out to the edges of the shores and touched the fingertips of the ocean—the ocean has never been touched a body as fluid as itself and it seemed that the ocean was delighted to meet one of its kind, a gentler version of itself. It was touched by the innocent toddling water streams.

Seaweed appeared and decorated the beaches, introducing a fresh new life on the coast and a tastier oceanic scent that was no longer just bluntly saline and dead. Long lines of coral spawn slick crawled on the calm surface of the ocean. The spawn connected the coast with the horizon in every direction, drawing a massive coral shape on the ocean's surface. Next, armies of plankton marched to the island's shores, followed by fleets of fly fish, bonitos, marlins, and sea turtles. Shadows of birds flying over the different schools of fish crowded the surface of the ocean.

One night, LaKhi ran to alert the others, pointing to the ocean with great excitement. He wanted them to witness the sight of waves magically lit in bright blue lights. The islanders, except for AiYi, had never seen the ocean being inscrutable and mystical as such. Today, the sea was filled with bright blue stars and calmly reflected the moon in perfection. Every wave was spectacular in its own way. The four islanders walked along the beach in silence. No one laughed or giggled. They just followed the waves as they flipped and tossed bright blue dots of light. The four islanders settled on the beach right in front of a big sunken rock. They spent the rest of the night watching the waves hit and light up the rocks until the sun came out and the bright blue light faded into the depth of the ocean.

After the festive migration of crabs and plovers, the island was further invaded by millions of golden and red wandering glider dragonflies chased by thousands of blue-cheeked bee-eaters and followed by thousands of rollers. Like colourful confetti, the sky was crowded with millions of creatures that twirled, manoeuvred, dipped, and soared. LaKhi and NooaKhi ran around like children while the birds forced the dragonflies to land on the ground for the two young men to chase and taste. When the restless birds and bugs got tired, they landed across the curves and edges of the rocky mountains. Many dragonflies left their larvae to grow in the many ponds that the island now hosted. The bee-eaters and the rollers then nested close to the ponds inside mountainous cracks and pores. The birds built their nest with dried seaweed. NooaKhi and LaKhi did not mind the birds' pecking while they shamelessly stole many eggs from the nests they found around the edges of the rocky mountains.

Green and brown algae appeared in ponds and crawled out of the water into the island's grey, red and brown rocks. The algae stayed fresh for insects, lizards, and crabs to feed on.

Birds carried and dropped seeds onto the island, leaving small gifts and remedies that later sprouted and made more life. Small green grasses and weeds started to grow and cover the dunes and mountains of the island. Some larger spots were pleasantly interrupted by patterns of tiny yellow flowers with a touch of a few white ones. The wind carried all sorts of swarms at night. The sun revealed the island's newcomers early every morning. More insects started to appear, more beetles and worms, and more wasps and bees built nests and hives under the shadows of the rocks.

Everything that moved, was food. Every life offered by land, sky, and sea was offered by the island to the islanders to fill their mouths and bellies. Poison was yet foreign. LaKhi and NooaKhi's curiosity had no limits. The two scouted the giant rocky beds looking for new forms of life. They saw a creamy yellow rock covered by bees, hanging down and hiding inside the shades of a small red rock hollow. The two climbed inside the hollow. Reached out to the soft beehive and picked it off the red rock. Bees flew everywhere and attacked the two islanders. The two young men's skins were too thick and dead already. Still their skins tingled, itched, and annoyed. They passed over the comb to each other and licked the liquid that covered their fingers. It was the purest taste of pleasure. A flavour that was most foreign for all the islanders and too powerful for AiYi's and SeeKa's taste buds. Every time AiYi got a chunk of the crumbling sweet, sticky honeycombs, she felt like her eyes would grow again in their sockets. SeeKa whined and nagged LaKhi for more; it was her new craving. She woke him up in the middle of the night several times, begging him to look for more honeycombs.

The sea too was apologizing, NooaKhi thought. It was not acting in the grumpy and stingy manner it had done in the past. Instead, its waves became calmer and the seawater sweeter and more transparent. Islanders could walk beside the shores comfortably and see squids and fish under the water from a distance. The sea became more caring and generous now, throwing out crabs, fish, shrimps, and squids into the small water pods and large rock pores across the shore. The sea made it easy for islanders to catch the food they desired. The tides were smooth and friendly, like a fishing companion that uncovered more squids and crabs for the islanders to easily pick by hand.

The island was as lively as a curious, unthreatened plover chick playing with sea shells on the beach on an early morning. It was also breathing calmly like a meditating, loving grandmother, enjoying the sight of her grandchildren. Like a growing foetus, there were significant milestones of progress and change taking place miraculously every day. And the islanders had to improvise, adapt, and innovate. Every week, they had to learn new hunting skills and tools, and new ways to prey upon the island's new tenants. LaKhi noticed the change in the tide. He took advantage of low tide and walked around the rock formations on the beach looking for trapped squids and fish that he could squeeze out with his toes. SeeKa used the leftovers of dead birds to lure crabs to the entrance of the cave. NooaKhi used dried seaweed to decorate his sleeping spot, a technique he learnt from the birds that built numerous nests out of seaweeds around the island.

AiYi, on the other hand, collected clams and shells and piled her treasures next to KaiKa's body. She was in an originality contest of her own against the island.

The islanders began to use the calm sea waters to defecate and avoid the odour. They bathed more often in freshwater ponds and quickly noticed how flies had started losing interest in their now clean bodies. Their skin and hair were getting cleaner and softer than ever. Their smiles and laughter were more frequent too. The islanders shifted from their nocturnal hunts to more diurnal ones. They started to enjoy better, and longer sleep at night.

Seven full moons passed, and there was a total absence of sandstorms and tornadoes. SeeKa felt every move her child was making. She was relieved and happy. The baby she carried was alive, restless, and full of energy. She did not need KaiKa anymore to comfort her about her child's well-being.

* * *

With every great day that passed, in what had become Green Island, NooaKhi gained more and more confidence in himself as the chief of his little tribe of four. His people were neither hungry nor thirsty anymore. Neither bored nor as anxious as they used to be. They had transformed from mice that kept close to their burrows into white-belly plovers that flew and walked and roamed courageously around the island. They all were stronger, felt more dazzling, and were safe under NooaKhi's reign. KaiKa's death brought life to the rest of the islanders, NooaKhi believed. They should be grateful for his glorious victory.

NooaKhi was surprised by his performance as the chief of his tribe. He was kind to all three islanders and his temper was calmer than before. They gathered around him every night. They offered him food whenever they caught something. They passed by him before taking their strolls. They did all that without him dictating these new norms. They just paid him the respect he always wanted, involuntarily. And with every hunt and every catch, NooaKhi abundantly shared food equally with the other islanders. There were no rankings nor hierarchical rules to follow when eating or drinking water. He gave them all full liberty and unlimited access to the water in the ponds. No permissions were needed to drink and eat.

Free food and water for all. And ever since KaiKa's death, he
did not aggressively lay his hands on anyone. Did not bite
any hand or shoulder and did not slap anyone's head or neck.
LaKhi thought of him as more impartial than KaiKa was.

LaKhi treated NooaKhi the way he had treated KaiKa, like
a rightful leader. He worked hard to impress him. Though
there were no instructions to follow, LaKhi waited for
NooaKhi's orders to obey. SeeKa, too, respected NooaKhi.
She quietly moaned and whined around him in pregnancy
pain and smiled when he caught her eye as she played with
LaKhi. SeeKa did not steal any food anymore.

Meanwhile, AiYi was still afraid of NooaKhi. She accepted
his generosity and all the food he shared and was not as
hesitant as she used to be. But she was still grieving and did
not smile as much as the rest. She had not forgotten KaiKa's
final voice before she had been killed by NooaKhi's hands in
the pond. The little girl missed KaiKa's touch and the feeling
of sleeping in her arms. AiYi continued to sleep in KaiKa's
ruins, even though the sand beds where her scent was once
had been wiped off completely.

* * *

SeeKa's stomach was as big and round as the sun.

All tribe members were excited to know what the gender
of the new islander would be, and they were more protective
and kinder to SeeKa. There was a mother in the making
among them. Their feelings towards her reminded them of
the warmth and unconditional love they had received from
their mothers.

While NooaKhi and LaKhi now believed that silence was
the sole reason for the absence of Sand monsters, SeeKa
believed in a different cause. She believed that she would
be giving birth to a special girl. She thought that the island
was only behaving exceptionally well in preparation for her
child's reception. She had a feeling that the child she was
carrying was a good omen to herself, LaKhi, and the fate of

the islanders. She started to believe that her child had all the special powers that calmed down the island and the raging waves that surrounded it. Her daughter had invited the rain, plovers, crabs, dragonflies, rollers, fish, and beautiful white clouds. She believed that all the magical blue lights the waves made at night were just a calling to her child. Her baby girl would grow old and read sand, the sun, the waves, the birds, and everything that was becoming green. Her baby girl would become the mother of all mothers. The first queen of Green Island.

The pain SeeKa had to bear was worsening every day. Though she was excited to meet her future queen and wanted her to quickly emerge from her belly, she still felt that her child was safest inside her. Even though the island was not the Sand Island she once knew, there was no NooaKhi in her womb, she thought. SeeKa was getting anxious that her womb was a better mother than her arms and breasts would be. SeeKa felt confident knowing how reliant her womb was but was yet to explore how reliant her breasts could be.

SeeKa was missing singing with LaKhi. She thought his voice would have performed the most alluring songs of hope. It was a shame that her daughter would not get a chance to hear the charming voice of her father singing, she thought. Yet, a mute father that was free to roam on a green island was better than a singing prisoner, she thought. Living in peace on an island that became green and gentle while carrying a child and feeling strong and healthy created strong desires in SeeKa to hear LaKhi sing her the song of hope. But also, her wishes were mixed with fear of taking her rewards for granted. What if she was wrong? She was afraid that Sand might strike hard at any moment because of their greed and lack of respect and appreciation. She feared the possibility of Sand being behind all the generous offerings of the sea and the sky. So as much as she was enjoying all her privileges, she was also threatened by them. She was still afraid that Green Island was just Sand Island in disguise, like a villain plotting a whole new style of terror.

One that is sudden. One that will wipe all four of them off the island, for good.

LaKhi, on the other hand, was running down a steep slope of love. His emotions towards SeeKa grew faster than the child she carried in her womb.

With discipline, he was fully dedicated to SeeKa's service. He woke up early every day, sprinted around the beach, and returned to SeeKa with a fresh catch. And if he were not out there hunting for food to feed SeeKa, he would be close to her, caressing her hair and belly, trying to get a reaction from his child. He saw the movement of the baby's elbow once and jumped and ran around the cave while the rest laughed at him. He walked SeeKa around the island sometimes, and he would run and come back to her with dozens of flowers and throw a shower of flowers on her body.

For LaKhi, silence had become the new pleasant form of song. He got used to listening to new sounds of nature, one that became more of a soothing piece of music than its preceding sounds of raging terror.

SeeKa's body, however, was not the only thing that was changing. The pain from carrying the child was irritating her day after day and peaked at night. LaKhi's presence was annoying her. She missed LaKhi's voice and singing. But now that LaKhi was silent, always running back and forth from the sea to where she sat with food, flowers, water, and seaweed, SeeKa was losing her appetite for LaKhi. Without his voice, LaKhi was beginning to seem more and more like NooaKhi. She was slowly untethering her way out of his charm.

* * *

Unlike her tribe members, AiYi could not enjoy the new colours introduced by the island's flowers, birds, and fish. Likewise, she could not enjoy the dozens of colours the insides of a single shell offered. However, she enjoyed the discoveries she made every time she touched the foreign shapes that shells and clams offered to her fingertips. She enjoyed the feeling of the smooth texture of the grass beneath her feet. The squishy surface of a squid's skin and tentacles. Soft rain showers drizzled on her body. The feeling of a child's kick from behind the taut skin of SeeKa's swollen stomach. The different sounds of birds chirping every morning and the tranquil sounds of the waves at night. The exotic and delicious taste of new animals. The magical taste of honeycomb. The smell of flowers and fresh air. All of that brought a whole new plethora of sensorial joys that she never knew existed.

Every day, AiYi wandered around the island on a cartography mission. She was building herself a new mental map of the island. With all the grass that grew around, she drew new lines that further articulated details to her map. Without sandstorms and tornadoes, Sand did not shift dunes and did not erase footsteps and pathways. Sand monsters were not there now to tear her maps into pieces anymore. AiYi felt that her map had never been safer to use.

SeeKa once took AiYi out to the beach and held her hand right over a crab hiding beneath the sand. She caught food in silence. AiYi's eye sockets did not quiver and were not bothered by any songs of hunger. SeeKa tapped AiYi's hand, and AiYi snatched the crab. Her first prey ever. LaKhi, on the other hand, took AiYi on one of his low tide walks. He led her to a pond that trapped an entire school of tiny fish. She danced over the fish with excitement. She had never been more confident and empowered.

She kept humming her songs in her head.

Not songs of hunger or thirst or fear or hope. Just the same song of gratitude she always hummed in her head. The same song she sang while walking with KaiKa on her sand-reading trips. The song she sang whenever KaiKa gave her food and allowed her to drink water. The song she hummed every time NooaKhi carried her on his shoulders and LaKhi offered her a sleeping spot. The song she sang whenever a sunny day passed with no sign of a sandstorm or tornado. The song she sang thousands of times, alone in her head. A song she sang while KaiKa was alive on Sand Island, and kept singing in silence to show her gratitude to Sand for keeping her alive on Green Island.

It was the only song she sang silently for this new avatar of the island. No one was allowed to sing out loud and no one but AiYi knew that songs could also be sung in silence.

* * *

It had been seven full moons since KaiKa's death.

Whenever SeeKa slept during the day, LaKhi spent time with NooaKhi. The two big boys raced each other across the island. They competed against each other in hunting games, burping games, and other silly meaningless games. LaKhi always appreciated his elder half-brother's presence and the entertainment that he offered.

Moreover, LaKhi started to see and admire new qualities in NooaKhi. The innovative drive NooaKhi had towards their new life and new ways to hunt and live on Green Island. The calmness and confidence he displayed when he came back from hunts. The hopefulness, generosity, and justice NooaKhi emitted when all four islanders gathered around food and water. NooaKhi had managed to acquire so many qualities as suddenly as the changes on the island. These qualities drove LaKhi to proudly call himself NooaKhi's second man in command. Unlike SeeKa's delusions, NooaKhi's reign was a reign of fathers.

NooaKhi believed that fathers are strong. Fathers are just and wise. Fathers are rich and could always provide. They seed the children inside their mothers and allow their growth. He believed that Sand feared fathers. He started to think that Sand had no respect for mothers and their desperate songs.

However, as the days and nights passed, LaKhi noticed that despite NooaKhi's fair treatment towards SeeKa and AiYi, he sometimes saw the girls with slight resentment. He gave them more food than they ever needed and granted them unlimited access to water. But he never invited them for walks. He never bothered to invite them to a game. He did not care to share his new skills with SeeKa as much as with LaKhi. He only laughed with LaKhi around. NooaKhi's supremacy was becoming more visible than before. He also did not hide his lust around the two girls. NooaKhi's uncanny smiles, anomalous acts of kindness, invasive cuddles at night, and his erections. NooaKhi could not hide his desire to have a child of his own.

Although LaKhi liked how NooaKhi led the tribe of four, he had started to become slightly nervous about NooaKhi's past. KaiKa's death still stood as evidence of what NooaKhi was capable of. LaKhi predicted that the mad NooaKhi could break out of his character. He was afraid that the same monster that lived inside NooaKhi and had killed KaiKa was just waiting for NooaKhi's nostrils to grow enough to leave NooaKhi's skull and kill someone else.

LaKhi only hoped that if NooaKhi ever snapped out of his current self, LaKhi would be there to protect SeeKa.

* * *

Not long after, the moment all four islanders had been looking forward to had come. SeeKa crouched between two large rocks with soft grass and wet seaweed beneath her. She was screaming in pain and pushing the child down and out of her womb. Her screams travelled to all edges of the island.

The sun was shining in the sky and giving the entire island the visibility it needed to witness the birth of SeeKa's child. The sea was respectfully calm and sent a cool breeze to SeeKa's path. Small scattered clouds drizzled and kept cleansing SeeKa's body. The island was welcoming the mother of mothers, SeeKa believed. Birds, fish, crabs, and squids were unbothered by the islanders while SeeKa was in labour. SeeKa gave all the creatures a grace period and a chance to give birth to their little ones and be left unbothered by the hunters.

LaKhi crouched in front of SeeKa with his hands over his forehead, gracelessly examining SeeKa's face and vagina while she flexed every muscle in her body. SeeKa painfully squeezed her body and screamed. Distracted by memories of KaiKa giving birth, SeeKa cried her sister's name. SeeKa wished for KaiKa to appear, grab the baby out of her body, and leave in silence. SeeKa pushed, squeezed, and howled, and memories of KaiKa vanished.

At the same time, NooaKhi stood nearby at the entrance of the caves, waiting for the child to appear. AiYi wandered around in circles close to SeeKa, not knowing what to do or how to help. She hummed her song silently and missed KaiKa.

It did not take long for the child's head to appear. Right before LaKhi attempted to examine the child's head, the child's whole body, the cord, and the ruptured placenta thoroughly and quickly slipped out of SeeKa's body. The newborn landed on its back into the soft bed of grass and seaweed that LaKhi had built, soaking it with placenta water.

SeeKa breathlessly and slowly kneeled. She laid down next to her child and realized she had given birth to a tiny boy. Not a girl. Not the omen she hoped for. Not the mother of mothers she expected. She was too tired to be distracted and protest. Too tired to revise her credence. She checked the baby's ears, arms, and legs, and counted his fingers and toes. Her baby boy calmed down instantly, and she surrendered and slept next to him.

LaKhi and the other two islanders now surrounded the calm newborn and his sleeping mother, all with giant silly smiles on their faces. They gathered around her, blocking the cool breeze for her and the child to warm up. Although NooaKhi was happy it was a boy, he did not spend much time around mother and child. He left the cave's grounds as soon as they slept. Indeed, it was the time of fathers, he thought. Meanwhile, AiYi was singing another song of gratitude all day long, a song she hoped one day would be the boy's first song to sing.

SeeKa woke up later that day to respond to the baby's cry. Her breasts were stiff, painful, and leaking milk. With his eyes closed shut, she wondered how the baby would learn to suck the milk out of her breasts. The baby boy moved his head restlessly. She noticed that the baby was trying to crawl into her breast with his head alone. It seemed like he already knew how to suckle. It was just a matter of helping him reach the spot from where the smell of milk oozed out. SeeKa adjusted the baby's body, and she brought his mouth closer to her nipple. At first, he struggled for a moment but quickly learnt to keep his mother's nipple settled in his mouth. The tiny baby boy was sucking into her breasts for milk as if he had been doing it for long. SeeKa stayed up all night watching her little boy and thinking. She now knew that the baby boy was not as vulnerable as she had thought. He was doing half the job. The boy was more intelligent than she thought. He was smart enough to prove to his mother that all her beliefs were wrong. He was not a magical girl but magical enough to be born alive.

SeeKa wondered, what happened to Sand. Why is the island so kind? Was KaiKa's songs the source of Sand's agony? Was NooaKhi's silence all that Sand wanted?

* * *

Both mother and the newborn spent the next few days together, quietly sleeping most of the time. It was as if the entire island was a bed that only carried the two of them. Everything they needed was served directly to their mouths. As much attention LaKhi was giving to his child and SeeKa, he did not get back from them. He became an invisible servant who kept his beloved SeeKa well-fed and the child safe and unbothered.

SeeKa wondered how and when babies detach from the placenta. She was afraid to touch the newborn's umbilical cord. She had to carry the baby and the placenta out under the sun and to the ocean; then, she rinsed the cord with seawater before she bathed the baby with freshwater from the ponds. After several days, the foul-smelling dark grey cord and placenta dried and fell off.

SeeKa had healthy, full breasts, and the newborn did not struggle to find his pacifying milk. However, SeeKa missed KaiKa deeply. She knew that if KaiKa were alive, she would have guided her into motherhood and childcare. KaiKa would have passed on a few skills and lessons on better reading a crying child, and how to attend to the child's needs. KaiKa would have discouraged her from certain habits and encouraged her to acquire new practises that could have made her stronger, wiser, and more attentive to the baby's needs. Instead, SeeKa had to explore and improvise with no direction or help. The two young men were no better than the fathers she knew. Neither could offer her the consultation she needed. The little blind girl was no better in this regard. All other islanders could not provide SeeKa the maternal support she needed. LaKhi sometimes picked up the crying child and wandered around to pacify the child. It worked a few times but did not work every time. AiYi held the child's tiny hands and foot to engage and soothe him, but that did not calm him. AiYi realized that holding on to the tiny baby's hands only did well for her benefit. The baby soothed AiYi more than she did the baby. NooaKhi just remained distant whenever the child cried. That was good enough support for SeeKa. All she ever wanted was for NooaKhi to be as far away as he could because of the tension he caused whenever he was around her baby. NooaKhi's new odd habits were making LaKhi and SeeKa nervous. Whenever he was around SeeKa and her breastfed child, he got an erection that he did not bother to hide. Furthermore, he would walk over to AiYi or LaKhi and order them to defuse his lusts while he watched SeeKa breastfeed the baby. He poked their bodies with tension and anger. And now that SeeKa had given birth, LaKhi became more worried and afraid than ever that SeeKa would become NooaKhi's targeted prey. Sleeping at night was a challenge for LaKhi as he had to guard SeeKa and his child.

On his third sleepless night, LaKhi saw NooaKhi indulging himself again. NooaKhi was erect as he walked and stood over SeeKa's head. She was sleeping while her child was feeding. He looked at her for a moment. Then his view was blocked by LaKhi's shadow and glowing eyes. Do not dare come any closer, LaKhi's eyes warned NooaKhi.

NooaKhi smiled through his yellow front teeth, and his nose puffed. He turned away from SeeKa and headed to where AiYi was sleeping. LaKhi followed him, his hands shaking. NooaKhi stood over AiYi and looked at her while she slept. LaKhi approached his brother, held his arm, and gently pulled him away from AiYi's resting spot. NooaKhi slapped LaKhi's hand, instructing LaKhi to walk away. NooaKhi wanted to be left alone with AiYi. The younger brother stepped away but stood close and carefully observed his older brother.

NooaKhi did not move. He looked at AiYi's small body lying down, sleeping under an almost full moon outside the cave on her sand bed. He looked back at LaKhi with a smirk on his face, then turned at AiYi and took a long lecherous look at her body. His erection was revived. Just as he kneeled and was reaching out to AiYi, LaKhi sprinted towards his elder half-brother and shoved him. Instead of falling away from AiYi, NooaKhi lost his balance and fell directly over AiYi's body. He laid his weight over AiYi's body. She instantly woke up scared and paralysed under NooaKhi's massive body. She was trying to figure out what was happening and whose weight she was beneath. She then recognized NooaKhi's body and breath, the same breathing sound she had heard after KaiKa was killed. She cried and sought for SeeKa and LaKhi's help in horror. She did not know his intentions yet but finding him on top of her was bizarre enough for her to panic and scream.

LaKhi jumped over NooaKhi and wrapped his arms around him, trying to pull him away from AiYi's body.

SeeKa woke up too and dashed towards the sound of AiYi's screams. She found LaKhi struggling against NooaKhi's weight. SeeKa jumped in and joined LaKhi, pulling NooaKhi off of AiYi's body. The two succeeded finally. NooaKhi now laid down, groaned, but did not resist. SeeKa stepped away, but LaKhi quickly wrapped his arms around NooaKhi's leg and tried to drag him away from AiYi's sleeping spot. This further angered NooaKhi and he kicked LaKhi's face. NooaKhi's heel aimed directly at LaKhi's left cheek and eye. The younger brother let go of his grip and fell backward and screamed in pain. LaKhi's hands reached to his cheek; it was bleeding, and the pain was burning.

* * *

All four islanders stood in the middle of the night. The air was humid and carried the baby's cries to AiYi's sleeping spot. The three older islanders looked at each other. None was sure how to end this or how it began. SeeKa gazed at NooaKhi. Sand had not disappeared yet, she thought. Sand walked amongst them. Sand had finally got the face of an islander. NooaKhi was Sand, and Sand was NooaKhi, she thought. SeeKa crouched and took a handful of sand, then threw it at NooaKhi. He did not move at all. She felt that the sand she had thrown at him went through him rather than being blocked by his face and chest. SeeKa leered at NooaKhi. She was sure now that the NooaKhi that stood in front of her was nothing but a Sand monster. The baby's cries got louder, and SeeKa immediately left the two islanders and ran towards her crying baby.

LaKhi held his face, strolled, and passed by NooaKhi and towards AiYi, who was still confused and moaning. He grabbed her shoulder, and she panicked. But then he had her closer to his chest for her to touch and smell. She calmed down, knowing that it was LaKhi giving her comfort. LaKhi then led AiYi to where SeeKa and the baby were resting.

None of the islanders slept that night, except for the baby. SeeKa and LaKhi stayed up with their eyes set on their baby and AiYi. While AiYi was still in shock, she realized that SeeKa and LaKhi had protected her from NooaKhi that night. She was not sure what NooaKhi intended to do with her. He killed KaiKa, and whatever plans he had were evil, she thought.

AiYi moved closer to SeeKa's body and cuddled her. She kept awake and sang her song of gratitude in her mind throughout the night.

* * *

The next day, NooaKhi was nowhere to be seen. LaKhi took the chance and walked AiYi out to the beach to catch some crabs. His face was bruised; his left eye was swollen shut so he could only see through his right eye. He wanted to bring some food to SeeKa but kept a close distance from the cave. His eye patrolled back and forth between the path leading to the cave and AiYi to ensure her safety. The little blind girl was already sitting, lying down, and crawling on the sand. She was playing and looking for seashells. She was silently singing her secret song.

LaKhi saw a large cast of crabs. So he went after it and started catching them one after the other.

AiYi's hands crawled on the sand and shuffled, looking for a new seashell to add to her collection. Her curious fingers dipped into the sand, lifted grains, took off, and plunged again. Her fingers acrobatically surveyed the sand, one spot after another. AiYi landed on a strange rock. Larger than her hand, lighter than a rock, with spines less violent than a crab's. Her finger slid into the rock surface and spiralled. She examined the smooth surface and looked for any signs of life. Her fingers did not encounter first contact with a new form of life. Here was yet another new form of the island. AiYi had just found her largest treasure. An abandoned giant conch shell. It was so big she could not hide it perfectly between her palms. She carried it close to her face. She shook, smelt, and tasted it. She touched its curvy harmless spines and slid her fingers inside it, enjoying the smooth surface of the inner shell. She held it close to her ear and listened to the wind passing through its hollowness. AiYi had a strange feeling passing through her ear and into her heart. AiYi felt with certainty the presence of KaiKa. As if she were behind her, looking right down at her. AiYi felt as if KaiKa was instructing her to not keep her song of gratitude a secret anymore. AiYi was pleased, for she had no desire to keep her song of gratitude a secret any longer. She was impressed by KaiKa's wisdom. KaiKa was a true mother, she thought. A mother would always know of her child's desires. Mothers were always encouraging. They knew better.

AiYi whispered, 'KaiKa?' and then heard footsteps behind her. AiYi stepped backward, turned around, and towards the footsteps she heard a moment ago. Nothing was there. AiYi whispered again, 'KaiKa.' There was no sound now other than the sounds of the ocean and flying fish in the distance.

AiYi returned to her spot, sat down, then brought the conch shell close to her mouth and softly started to sing her song of gratitude into the shell. She stopped after a few moments of singing. Listening to her voice singing again scared her a bit. She breathed for a few moments, gathered some courage, then sang the song of gratitude. She sang it louder this time.

The song was sung in harmony with the ocean's waves and the sound of the wind. AiYi was playing a solo conducted by the island. She was led to sing her song by nature. With every splash, she mimicked the waves. And when the wind carried grains of sand, AiYi mimicked the sounds it made. And between the waves and the wind, AiYi filled her song with her soft voice and long breaths of gratifying wails.

SeeKa was sleeping next to her baby. LaKhi was running around crabs. A wave made a splash. Another wave calmly pushed the water to LaKhi's feet and uncovered a crab from beneath the sand where it hid. The water pulled the crab and snatched it before LaKhi could catch it. Another wave, more significant, made a louder splash. LaKhi looked into the horizon that split the ocean from the sky. Another wave made a thumping splash. Then he noticed the camouflaging sound of a song. He heard AiYi's song of gratitude. He turned his head toward AiYi's voice and saw her sitting on the sand. Standing right behind her. unnoticed, was NooaKhi, holding a big rock in his hand.

LaKhi shouted 'AiYi!' and ran towards her.

But NooaKhi had already struck AiYi with the rock. A loud high-pitched scream escaped from AiYi's throat. NooaKhi had aimed to hit her face but struck her chest instead. He jumped at her and threw several punches at her face and body. Each punch interrupted her screams, and her voice faded into painful cries. With each punch, NooaKhi accused AiYi of being ungrateful to silence, ungracious to the Green Island, and disrespectful to his will. Her face was flaming and stinging. A flame she had once felt all over her head and body when she was trapped in the sandstorm as a child.

LaKhi threw himself on his half-brother and tried to stop his punches. But NooaKhi was unstoppable. AiYi let out a long cry. She twisted, pushed, kicked, and punched but was too small to push away NooaKhi's body. LaKhi abruptly held NooaKhi's legs pulling him away from AiYi. But with no luck. NooaKhi's weight felt twice as heavy as the night before. Finally, he lifted the rock that he had used to strike AiYi, stood off of the little blind girl, and struck LaKhi's bruised face.

LaKhi screamed in pain, fell to the ground, and twisted in pain. SeeKa, now awake, ran towards the commotion, carrying her crying baby in her arms. She rushed to AiYi's desperate pleas for help, cries that had travelled from the beach to where she was lying in the cave.

NooaKhi turned back to AiYi. He marched purposely towards her intending to end what he had started. AiYi was frozen in panic. She tried to move but went around in circles trying to find her way to safety. She screamed, desperately crying out to summon SeeKa or LaKhi. She knew they were all close. She just hoped that they were closer than NooaKhi.

AiYi stopped crying for a moment, breathing heavily, as the pain in her body went from total numbness to flaming stings. She was fuming. She stopped moving. And before NooaKhi could reach, AiYi started to howl the song of fury.

NooaKhi was panicking. He ran and jumped at AiYi and they both fell to the ground. His hands were stuck between his body and AiYi's and clutched into her arm. He aimed to cover her mouth to stop her from singing but struggled to pull his hands. She shouted, 'NooaKhi!' On hearing his name, NooaKhi rolled away from AiYi who tried to crawl away and stand up again. NooaKhi swiftly held her waist and dropped her back to the ground. He took a handful of sand, swung his hands, and made an arch of scattered sand above his head. He shoved his sand-filled hand into AiYi's mouth and forced three of his long hardened fingers down her throat.

AiYi dug her teeth into his fingers in desperation, but it was difficult because she was being suffocated. The moment AiYi let go, NooaKhi screamed in pain and pulled out his hands. There was blood all over. AiYi had exposed the bones in two of his three bitten fingers.

Meanwhile, SeeKa desperately tried to reach out to AiYi but LaKhi had blocked her path. When he heard AiYi's song of fury, he forcefully pulled back SeeKa towards the cave. The waves were now splashing with aggression. The nervous ocean was becoming hysterical. LaKhi was afraid of what might turn Green Island into Sand again. LaKhi firmly wrapped his arms around SeeKa and the baby. SeeKa twisted, trying to escape from his grip. She demanded to save AiYi from NooaKhi. But LaKhi disregarded her demands and kept pushing her back to the cave. SeeKa resisted and ordered LaKhi to stop. He did, but only to point at the horizon and the raging ocean. SeeKa had always been aware of her superiority over LaKhi. She knew she was more powerful than him. However, she did not have enough drive to practice her power at that moment. So with her eyes set on her son, she decided to let LaKhi lead her into his will. SeeKa gave up her fight. They both ran away towards the cave.

When NooaKhi was distracted by his fingers, AiYi started to wail the song of fury again. It brought his attention back to AiYi and he wrapped his hands around her neck and pressed it against the ground.

In the distance, LaKhi left his son and SeeKa at the cave entrance and was running back towards NooaKhi and AiYi. Suddenly he saw the sun disappearing above the sky. He froze. There was a gigantic ugly dark cloud approaching. A sandstorm was on its way. LaKhi silently ran back to the cave and, with SeeKa, started to bury the small entrance with rocks.

With a mouth full of sand, AiYi kept singing the song of fury. She kicked, punched, and paused only to grasp some more air, sing, and howl louder.

By now NooaKhi too had tired. A couple of AiYi's kicks had hurt his knees. He adjusted his position, raised his hips away from AiYi's legs and knees. He sat on her stomach with his upper body leaning toward AiYi's neck and face. NooaKhi depended on his entire weight to do the rest of the job. His head looked down towards the top of her head.

AiYi stopped singing. Then, stopped kicking. But NooaKhi did not release her yet. Even though she was motionless, he stayed right on top with his hands pressing hard. Then, with his hands still wrapped around AiYi's neck, NooaKhi leaned back to see AiYi's face. He froze in his position, breathing through his nose, hard and quick.

All noise disappeared. The ocean was silent.

The ugly dark cloud was right above NooaKhi and AiYi. He listened to the sound of his sweat dropping and striking AiYi's face. One drop. Then the second.

In an instant, the sandstorm plummeted to the ground and trapped NooaKhi who had no chance to flee. NooaKhi ran in circles with his eyes closed. He was suffocating and could feel his skin peeling. He tried to find his way to the caves but instead ran towards the raging sea.

When he walked into the water, he screamed in pain like he was being stung to death. Then a cold wave smashed into NooaKhi's body. He went limp and was pulled into the ocean's gut. NooaKhi was dead.

* * *

AiYi was dead too.

Yet her heart was pounding, and she was breathing in the dark.

Chapter Six
The Song of Truth

I am the very,
very, very old man
of the island.
I
am
the island.
I have no sons, had no daughters, and no treasures !
I hear you sing songs
that turn me into a very,
very, young strong man.
Your songs make me
strong enough
to bring you
justice.

Your	songs
make	magic
that	keeps
us all	alive.

AiYi had died a moment ago, yet here she was standing up, in total darkness.

She could feel her weight and the smooth surface below her feet. She was not standing on sand or grass or anything that felt like her sleeping spot. She was not standing over any familiar rock. The sound of the ocean seemed to be coming from a place far from her sleeping spot where she had died.

She was breathing, and her heart was beating fast. AiYi listened carefully to her breath, trying to make sense of this unfamiliar territory of darkness.

A few moments before standing on the smooth surface, alive again, AiYi had been submerged in terror and panic. Her mouth had been filled with sand. She had felt an excruciating pain in her neck and throat; lungs burnt and collapsing, desperately begging for air; jaws overstretched and fatigued. But now, all the pain she had felt was gone. All the terror and noise had vanished completely as if it had never happened.

AiYi touched her neck, looking for the painful bruises NooaKhi had left, but she did not find any trace. She felt her face. Her cheeks were soft and undisturbed by excess skin and the scars she had always had since she was a child. Was it a dream? She wondered. It cannot be a dream. Dreams were never painful, she told herself.

Her heart pounded when she felt something alien on her face; two large tumours nested over her eyes sockets, beneath her eyelids. As she examined the tumours, one eyelid sneaked in a shimmer of light to one of her perfectly formed eyes. She startled and screamed, her breath coming in quick, short gasps.

AiYi twirled around herself and walked in a circle, then ran into a wall. She touched the wall's surface with both hands. So smooth and perfectly flat. Never had she ever felt a surface as perfect as this one was.

Her hands were unconsciously placed on both sides of her head, touching her complete pair of ears covered under a thick hair that she had never had. She could not find the damaged scalp she grew up with.

The bewildered AiYi moved her eyelid muscles, flickering them while still closed. Then, she opened her eyes. And there it was—that first light seeping in through her unaccustomed eyes.

Afraid of the light, AiYi quickly shut them, then squinted for a few moments before finally opening them again.

She could see now. A wall in front of her. So high and so vast.

She placed her hands on the wall and started walking, sliding along her hands as she moved. When she reached the end of the wall, her hands were blocked by a bent on the wall. She slowly turned to the left. She was now standing on a terrace that overlooked one side of the island. She could not recognize the ocean or anything that stood between her feet and the horizon. Suddenly, she sensed a movement to her left. She looked to her left. An old man and a young woman were standing opposite her in a large rectangular chamber with three walls and a terrace. Alarmed, AiYi stumbled back from the man and the woman and leaned against one of the chamber's walls.

She had never had a dream like this before. Her breathing was still fast and shallow.

AiYi watched them as the old man softly held the young woman's arm and led her to the other end of the chamber, across from where AiYi was standing. The young woman was smiling but her tear-filled eyes were fixed on AiYi's face.

AiYi stood there frozen, carefully watching the two unfamiliar persons and trying to make sense of the strange reality that she perceived through her brand new eyes.

The old man raised his hand, and a doorway appeared out of nowhere. The door opened to what seemed to be stairs that led to an endless tunnel.

'It's time to go,' the man said to the young woman. AiYi could not hear the old man's voice. His lips did not move either.

The young woman resisted. Her eyes were still fixed on AiYi's face and her hand reached out towards AiYi. The young woman wanted to touch AiYi.

The old man softly held the young woman's face, turned it towards him, and whispered, 'Listen to me.' The young woman's eyes finally got distracted. She looked at him, and he smiled and advised the young woman, 'You must go now. The more I keep the door open, the more tired I become. Please... go.'

The young woman was tempted to turn and look at AiYi, but the old man did not allow it and assured with a weakened voice, 'You will see her sooner than you think, and you will hug her as much as you want. There's a lot of love behind this door. Now go! YOU MUST GO NOW!'

The old man lowered his exhausted arm and just as the young woman finally entered the opening, the door vanished into the wall.

AiYi stood fixed at her spot, too stunned to react. She could not recognize the young woman but recognized the motherly smile on her face. She felt calmer and started to breathe more steadily.

The old man, on the other hand, was drained and felt heavy. He slowly approached AiYi and examined her face from a short distance. AiYi looked at him cautiously but she was not afraid anymore.

The man had an abnormally big round head for a short man. He was thin, yet his belly was large and round. His long white twisted beard blended into his chest hair and was tied to his pubic hair like a string instrument. Ironically, he had no hair on his scalp but had thick long white eyebrows that partially covered his bright smiling eyes and partly flew around wildly, covering his forehead. Wrinkles, age spots, and thick purple veins covered his legs and hands. The prominent creases on his cheeks and eyes amplified the warm, comforting smile on his face.

The old man came closer to AiYi, who was now shivering, and touched her forehead. Then, without moving his lips, he spoke 'AiYi,' and she heard his deep soothing fatherly voice. 'My beloved little blind girl.'

He looked up at the chamber's ceiling, and AiYi followed his line of sight. He squinted and said, 'You sang twenty-five thousand and one hundred, and sixty-three songs. Fourteen thousand and three hundred and twenty-two songs of thirst. Six thousand and eight hundred and forty-eight songs of hunger. Eight hundred and thirty-five songs of fear. Two songs of fury. One song of hope. And the three thousand and one hundred and fifty-five songs no one heard other than me. The songs of gratitude you sang for the island; the songs you sang for me.'

AiYi was surprised that she understood everything he said as if each word he spoke out loud already existed in her memory but was sleeping in her head only to be woken up by his voice.

The very old man was interrupted by the abrupt entrance of a young man carried by Sand through the terrace. The young man floated into the chamber motionless and was dropped roughly on his face. He remained motionless on the ground. Sand respectfully kneeled to the old man of the chamber whose eyes were disrespectfully shut. Sand rose and left the chamber.

The interrupted old man pointed at the young man's body, then looked at AiYi. Finally, he sighed, 'NooaKhi... This one here sang fourteen thousand and two hundred and thirty-seven songs. Seven thousand and two hundred and sixty-eight songs of thirst. Five thousand and two hundred and forty-three songs of hunger. One thousand and seven hundred and twenty-six songs of fear. Of which, eleven thousand and nine hundred and seventy-six songs were torture to my ear. He was unnecessarily loud and only sang to make noise. I only liked the songs he sang when he was a little boy.... He was a good boy. He was a good man too, with so many good intentions. Before he turned into a murderer.'

The old man sighed softly. 'You should not be worried about him. He will remain here until I gather enough power to send him away to join the Sand monsters. But now... I am drained. I need to rest, my beloved girl. I need a few sunsets to see and a few bird songs to hear. Then... I can tell you my story.'

The old man laid down on the terrace with his head facing the sea and leaning over his hand.

AiYi followed him, stood on the ground next to the old man, and crossed her legs facing the sea.

* * *

AiYi spent a few days resting with the old man, enjoying the chamber's terrace view. The terrace extended around the three walls of the chamber where AiYi could enjoy the full view of the island and its never-ending horizon.

She had no expectations of what lay ahead. Neither could she anticipate her new senses nor predict the old man. She was in no rush for him to wake up. She was not hungry, thirsty, or afraid. Instead, she felt like she was in a fantastic dream from which she did not want to wake.

At first, she had thought that colours were living beings that had distinguished sounds—every red chirped, green hissed, blue softly roared, yellow calmly purred, and black stayed silent. Then she realized that some yellow buzzed rather than purred, some blue swooshed rather than roared. So AiYi had to rethink, conclude, and adjust to the idea that a single colour was capable of making a spectrum of sounds.

AiYi then thought that shapes might be better at categorizing sounds since colours had failed to do so. But she quickly concluded that each shape could also sing thousands and thousands of different songs, make thousands and thousands of other noises, and be silent too.

AiYi spent some time watching birds and associating the different sounds she already knew with the different birds she was able to see. The sounds she recognized once while alive now had colour, shape, and more character. She could also see the birds that clicked and those that boomed, the ones that scratched, and those that clacked. She realized that those that flapped their wings with pride in darkness were large, under the sunlight. And those that were discrete were small and adorable. All those sounds did not come from a single source or kind but many. She was fascinated by all the different types of birds that passed by her view.

She also studied how motion could explain the sounds that made up the world she knew once. She noticed that sounds that walked on the ground were different from sounds that flew. The sound of the same chirp was slightly different when it came from the land than from the air. And she thought of sounds as light as the wind and sounds as heavy as rocks. The wind made a louder sound than a silent sitting rock. She concluded that sound and motion had stronger ties than sound and colours or shapes.

With each realization, words woke up and queued excitedly in her mind waiting for their turn to be spoken, heard, or thought of again, and for the old man to hold them up like pictures and tell a story.

She only disturbed the old man once—the dawn after she appeared in his chamber. While she was enjoying the sight and movement of the ocean's waves on the horizon at dawn, she was stunned by the first glimpse of the tip of the sun coming out of the sea. She slapped the old man's head and pointed at the rising sun. The old man smiled and comforted her. 'One of the world's wonders. Calm down. The sun gives purpose to your new eyes... Sit, my girl. Enjoy it.'

By the time the sun rose and parted from the ocean, AiYi felt a fresh kind of peace and a strange bittersweet sort of content. Then later at night, AiYi was further stunned by the waves glowing in the dark night. Her eyes were enchanted and could not leave the sight of the mesmerizing glow that danced beneath the surface of the ocean's water.

With every fresh emotion, words woke up and queued in her mind waiting for AiYi to be brave enough to speak her first words.

* * *

Three sunrises went by. AiYi was crouching on the edge of the terrace, looking at a flock of birds flying over the ocean.

The old man stood up, and through his unspoken words, he politely asked AiYi, 'Sit down, my beloved girl. Let me tell you my story.'

AiYi smiled. With excitement, she sat down and listened carefully.

The old man was now sitting next to AiYi, and they both faced the terrace. He took a deep breath before he started telling his story.

'This beautiful island. This island of sand. It was the greenest island one could find in the entire big blue ocean... full of life.'

The old man made a dreamy face and disclosed, 'I was the only islander living on this island... For so long. I lived here alone in peace. I lived the life of a prisoner in this chamber... I could not leave the chamber, but I could see the entire island from this terrace.'

A warm fatherly giggle escaped his mouth, and he opened his eyes wide and lowered his voice as if he was telling AiYi a secret. 'I would lie if I said that I was completely alone. I made friends with all kinds of birds.'

The old man suddenly stood and ran to one of the chambers' corners and pointed to the ground. 'Curious plovers and terns came to my terrace. They rested here to digest their meals, and spread their oceanic aroma into my chamber.'

AiYi giggled at how fast the man ran to the end of the chamber. The old man raised his hands, reaching out to the sea, and continued, 'Noisy noddies woke me up and watched sunrises with me. Jaunty warblers and red fodies passed by my terrace and sang songs to each other. A few playful black parrots and parakeets lived in my chamber. I gave some of the parrots names and mourned their death too.'

The old man kept running from one corner to another while citing lines he had cited thousands and thousands of times before. 'Blue pigeons came over and nested on my terrace. I saw their squabs hatch and be taken care of by their parents until they were ready to fly away, knowing that one day they would come back again and build their nests around me, prepared to be parents of a whole new band of squabs. Rollers, paradise flycatchers, scoop owls, drongos, pink-backed pelicans, and many other migrating birds passed by my terrace.

'Some came back again, and most flew away and never came back. Whales, dugongs, dolphins, and orcas waved at me from the shore. I heard their playful clicks and whistles and their mighty songs too. They travelled away every year and came back here singing new songs I had not heard before.

'Old sea turtles appeared on the shore and nodded to me. "Hello young man!" they said. They dropped their eggs and nodded at me again before they left. "See you next year!" they said.'

The old man laid down on his chest, leaning close to the edge of the terrace with his face resting on his hands, and turned towards AiYi and asserted, 'I kept an eye on their eggs until they hatched. Those tiny little turtles never looked at me, though. They always came back again when they were big enough to lay their eggs on the island. I could not tell them apart. But they were all my friends.'

The old man leaped like a frog and attempted to jump again but stopped to catch his breath. He crawled slowly on his elbows next to AiYi and crossed his legs, then continued, 'Colourful tiny frogs, wolf snakes, geckos, skinks, chameleons, and lizards sneaked into my hidden chamber. I did not like those naughty crawlers as much as I liked the birds. I had to ask them to stay away and let me be.

'Colonies of flying foxes swung upside down and ate fruits on tree branches that grew next to my chamber. They were too noisy! But I liked them. They were fun to watch. Small mice chased each other into this chamber, and I welcomed them all.'

The old man raised his right hand, then slapped his left hand in a loud clap, and continued. 'Some were chased by owls and eaten inside my chamber.'

AiYi looked shaken by the old man's clap and voice.

The old man softened his voice and assured, 'I would not interfere with them... I would never interfere with nature.'

The old man stood up again, walked to the edge of the terrace, and continued, 'Bees and wasps built and abandoned beehives and nests on tree branches close to the terrace.

The breeze blew into my way from time to time.'

The old man swung and lightly twirled. 'The long songs of nature played day and night, and I danced alone on my terrace. The song nature sang was healing and peaceful. It kept me young for so long.'

The old man stopped, shook away his dizziness, and then sat crossed-legged facing AiYi. He tilted his head and smiled. 'The song of nature played for so long. Long enough that I forgot what my name was. I forgot how I ended up here in this chamber. I stopped dancing to the charming songs of nature. I sat down and remained sitting on the ground with my eyes set on the shore.'

Next, the old man turned to sit next to AiYi. He faced the sea and continued: 'I spent a very long time just watching the sun rising and floating over my head. I watched it disappear behind my back, then rise again. I have seen thousands and thousands of sunrises. They were all the same. My mind was thoughtless. I bet the trees had more thoughts than I did.'

The old man suddenly clapped and excitedly said, 'One day! My enduring peace was finally interrupted when I heard a new sound approaching the island. I jumped and ran around my terrace and danced! It was the happiest day of my life. Nearly a dozen of your ancestors sailed to my island on a wooden boat. They were the first settlers of Green Island.

'They looked nothing like you, AiYi. They were tall and strong. They looked happy and full of life. They were covered with gold and colourful clothes.'

With every word the old man used to describe AiYi's ancestor, his hands and eyes moved beyond his body like marionettes supporting his act.

'No bird was as colourful as your ancestors. No whale was as giant as their boats. And no ant or bee was as hardworking and restless as they were. They docked and descended onto my island, and they came closer into the heart of my island.'

The old man was now standing at the edge of his terrace. He pointed to a nearby spot, and exclaimed, 'They came as close as here! I got to see their faces, I thought. They had different faces. Men. Women. And a few children. Each had a face of his own. They made me wonder what my face looks like. I still wonder...'

The old man paused. He walked around AiYi with his hands on his chin, repeating the question over and over. 'What does my face look like? What does my face look like? What does my face look like?'

AiYi wanted to describe his face for him, but she was neither capable of expressing a face yet nor courageous enough to use her voice. The old man looked at her and snapped his finger in front of her confused face. 'As your ancestors settled in, I began to observe them, day and night from my invisible terrace—unnoticed and undiscovered. They were pleasant to watch and more enjoyable to listen to. My new guests were more intelligent and curious than the mice I knew. More harmonious than the fodies I heard. More careful than the sneaky snakes. And more respectful than the silly, noisy flying foxes.'

The old man softened his voice and embraced himself. 'They were kind to my island too.'

He pointed out to the island with his palm open and said, 'They scouted the entire island and gave names to every bird, every rodent, and every plant. I learnt from them that a tern was called a tern, that the flying fox was actually a bat and not a bird, which made me wonder what a fox looked like!'

The old man drifted away for a bit, lost in thought. Then he pondered aloud. 'And what does my face look like? What does my face look like?'

Then snapping out of his reverie, the old man jumped and clapped. 'And I learnt from them that a whale is not a fish! They were right! Whales do not lay eggs as fish do. I was fascinated by their knowledge and more fascinated by their skills.

'The fire they harnessed.

'The animals they milked.

'And all the vegetables they farmed and fruits they harvested.

'And all the huts they have built.'

The old man started to swing. He used his hands like a musical instrument, and chanted, 'And the arts! Their crafts. The cooking and the baking! They made the most delicious smells with their fire and their ovens. The smell of bread. I never tasted it, but it smelled so good.

'And the dancing too!

'And the stories they told each other.

'And the singing! They were kind to each other with their songs. During the day, they worked with each other and cared for one another, and sang together. And during the night, they loved one another and sang together. Their songs were magical.

'They were also stronger and mightier as they sang in unison, building structures and farming the land. When a child cried, a mother would sing a song that calmed the child and put him to sleep. Two would transform into lovers after singing to each other in the night away from the rest. The entire tribe sang for the same two lovers and transformed the lovers into parents who then sang to their children.'

The old man's voice softened as he confessed, 'Every time the newly settled islanders sang, I listened in envy. Everyone had a song sung to them. But they never sang a song for me.'

The old man got closer to AiYi, raised his eyebrows, and told a story, 'One night while everyone was sleeping, the song of nature was interrupted by a strange sound. A man was weeping in the middle of the night. His name was MaSi. He was sitting there next to his own body crying.

'I watched. I was puzzled. Someone other than me touched by magic?

'After sunrise, MaSi left the cave and walked like a blind man on the island. He entered his village and walked crying among other islanders, but no one could see him. He left no

footprints behind. And no one could hear him weep. Like me, touched by magic.

'I stepped into my terrace and called his name. I spent all day shouting his name. He could not hear my voice and kept walking in his own darkness.

'After many days and nights of walking around, MaSi finally stepped into my hidden chamber. He saw me. He was horrified by my existence. I was excited; he validated my existence. Once he calmed down, we talked for a long time in my chamber. He told me his story. He had gold, a pretty wife, and wonderful children. He was killed by his brother who wanted to steal MaSi's gold, marry MaSi's wife, and become a father to MaSi's children. He was angry about his death and outraged by his brother. He wanted justice. He wanted revenge. He wanted another chance to live. He wanted to be with the family he loved, and dance with them while they sang to each other.

'He made me think. He made me wonder. Why am I not loved? Could I have a song of my own? How could I have someone sing for me? I wanted to be loved. I wanted songs to be sung to me.'

The old man was distracted by his thoughts. His eyes glided away before landing back on AiYi. 'One day, MaSi asked me how long I had been here alone on the island? So I told him.

'I have been around for thousands of years. I know every tree, every bird, every rock, and every stream. I explained how the song of nature was the reason I had stayed young for so long. He started to envy me. He wished that he could live on the island, forever young. He wished that his wife and children and parents could live forever with him on that island.

'I had a strong desire to make MaSi's wish come true. I felt a strange tingling in my hands. I raised my hands and with the tip of my fingers drew a portal on the wall. A door appeared out of nowhere for the very first time. One that I had never seen before.

'Strangely, I knew exactly where that door would lead MaSi to. It was the door to the Evergreen Island of Eternity. The portal was heavy to keep open. I commanded MaSi to go in immediately! But he refused. He said he would not go anywhere before he saw the death of his brother with his own eyes.

'I promised him. He would live in eternal peace once he went into the portal. I promised to erase all the hate and anger he had for his brother. I promised that he would forget that he ever had a brother and that the pain he felt would never be his.

'Yet he refused! He wanted to stick around in the chamber. He would never rest in peace knowing his brother was alive. He would never rest in peace knowing his wife might fall in love with his brother. He was worried his children would forget him. He worried that his brother would replace all the good memories his wife and children had of him. He said he would only rest in peace once he saw his brother suffer forever.'

The old man lifted his white beard in front of AiYi's face, opened his eyes wide, and cried, 'MaSi pointed at my face. "Look!" he said. "Your beard. It's turning white!"'

The old man lifted his hands and wailed, 'My beard and the back of my arms and the rest of my body were turning old so quickly. The magic I used to keep the portal open was draining my youth suddenly. I was getting tired. We both realized the magic I made came in exchange for my youth.

'While carrying the weight of the portal, I wanted love. I needed a song. All I wanted was songs to be sung for me.

'I promised to deliver justice to MaSi and all other good islanders who lived their lives harmlessly on the island. But, in exchange for songs. Songs would make me young again. Songs would make me open the portal for everyone who walked into my chamber—those who were good to the island, those who sang to me with their hearts. They would all be greeted and guided to an Evergreen Island of Eternity to live in peace forever.

'MaSi enquired about his brother. He said, "What would happen to my brother?"'

The old man closed his eyes. He remained silent for a moment, then opened his eyes, looked straight into AiYi's, and confessed, 'I promised MaSi that those who are as evil as your brother, those who harm my island, those who kill, those who deceive, who steal, who harm others, and those who are merciless, and those who are dissonant or do not want to sing—they all will be turned into Sand! In sandstorms and tornadoes, they shall forever be in terror and pain.'

The old man stopped and examined AiYi's face. She spoke her first word: 'Then?'

The old man confirmed. 'MaSi and I agreed. I instructed MaSi that the rest of the island's new settlers should never fight or kill. They should never talk to each other. And only sing songs for me, day and night.'

The old man's face wrinkled in distaste, 'They were noisy when they were not singing,' and swung his finger in front of AiYi's face. 'I explained to MaSi. Through songs, I will obtain powers that will lead the good singing islanders to peace and will be able to transform his brother and all other evil islanders into endlessly painful sandstorms and tornadoes.

'I promised MaSi that he would be the first to step a foot on Evergreen Island of Eternity and that his evil brother would be the first to suffer forever as Sand.

'But how can my people know of the deal we made— MaSi had asked me.

'I instructed him to walk in total darkness. To find a living dreaming body and deliver the deal we made by singing the song of truth into the ear of any living sleeping body.

'I promised him. Whoever received the song of truth would know of my existence and the deal we made. I begged him to go out and run. I was not sure if I could bear the pain of keeping the portal open. I was not sure if he would find me alive when he steps into the chamber again.'

The old man clapped and asserted in a rush, 'Immediately, MaSi went out of my chamber and ran towards his village.

He was blind and outraged by the betrayal of his brother. I must say. MaSi was the most frightening ghost that ever walked on this island!'

The old man clapped again, took a breath, then continued, 'After a few days—the most painful days I have ever lived—finally, MaSi navigated his way to find his father, the leader of the tribe. He followed his father and waited for him to sleep next to his mother. MaSi sang into his parents' ears. He delivered the truth of his own death and the details of my promise to him. Then he returned to my chamber and found me battling my own death.

'But as I promised, MaSi's parents woke up, instantly aware of the deal MaSi and I had made. They found MaSi's body in the cave stabbed with MaSi's brother's dagger. With great sorrow, the father executed his other son. And MaSi witnessed it all.

'MaSi saw his brother's corpse being carried and dropped off here in the chamber. His parents had followed their son's instructions and ordered everyone to never speak again. The tribe was instructed to only sing songs to me as long as they lived on my Green Island.

'They believed my word. They believed that the songs they would sing to me would lead them to an even greener, livelier peaceful eternity. They believed that the same songs would avenge all those wicked islanders among them.

'MaSi's mother sang me the first song ever. She sang me a song she used to sing to her two sons when they were still young boys.

'As if she gave birth to me—a birth that I witnessed—the mother's song transformed me into a powerful man in an instant. All the pain from carrying the portal's weight vanished. The portal became weightless.

'MaSi and I danced to my song that day. We clapped and ran in circles around MaSi's wicked brother, who was lying down on the ground, the way NooaKhi is lying here.

'When MaSi stopped dancing, he examined the portal. I encouraged him to jump into it but he refused. He wanted to see what would happen to his cruel brother first. I thought of the terror the brother had caused the day he murdered MaSi and pointed my hands towards the motionless cold corpse of MaSi's brother.

'The brother transformed into Sand and screamed in pain as he ran out of the chamber like a terrified injured animal. MaSi heard the pain his brother turned into. He looked at me and nodded, then walked into the portal. MaSi and the portal disappeared.'

The man of the chamber stretched his arms and adjusted his legs. He sat down next to AiYi on the ground and noticed that AiYi was distracted by the tip of the sun appearing on the horizon.

The two watched in silence as the sun emerged from the silky blue blankets of the calm ocean.

When the sun was complete, the old man resumed narrating his story but kept his eyes glued to the horizon.

'I enjoyed watching those islanders live in peace, build their village, hunt, trade, and dance. And most of all, I enjoyed the songs they sang for me. They gave birth to many children, and they lived long lives. I became younger, stronger, and more powerful every time they sang. I could hear every heartbeat on the island. I could see every stone, every leaf, every movement, every eyelash, and every dream they had ever had. The powers I earned through the songs were stronger than I had imagined. Nature continued singing soft songs but I had stopped paying attention to them.'

The old man shrugged. 'Why listen to them if I had delightful songs sung loudly just for me?'

The old man stood up, walked in front of AiYi in circles, and continued, 'Over the years, I noticed that the songs I thought were sung for me, were actually sung *to* me. They were not sung for me.

'Mothers sang. To be able to meet with the children they lost.

'Orphans sang. To see their mothers again.

'Widows sang. To reunite with the men they lost.

'Men sang. To keep their possessions after they die.

'The sick sang. To live a better life after death.

'The unfortunate sang. To be rich after death.

'Young girls sang. To find love and be loved.

'Old girls sang. To live in peace and not be forced to hide their love.

'Sinners sang. To redeem themselves and ask for forgiveness.

They had turned me into a merchant. They were all singing songs to me, asking for something in return. But no one sang a song *for* me anymore. Yet, I had to keep my promise. A song sung to me was still a song I had to count on. So I kept sending all those who sang to Evergreen Island of Eternity. Along the way, I also turned as much as half of the dead to raging thunderous Sand monsters to be tortured forever.' The old man was staring at NooaKhi as he spoke these words. But AiYi avoided looking at him.

'Small, cowardly sandstorms started to appear on the island. They barked at islanders and their children from a distance and sent terror to the children's hearts. The more islanders were turned to Sand, the larger and more monstrous, hungry, and courageous the sandstorms and tornadoes became. Children, women, and men started to sing the song of fear.'

The old man of the chamber clapped his hands and exclaimed, 'Finally!'

He looked into AiYi's round wide eyes and with great animation, he continued: Sandstorms and tornadoes grew so big that they started to tear the Green Island apart! Sandstorms wiped the small village huts out of the scalp of the island, stealing away the islanders' pets and crops, their bread, and all their food, pots and tools, their clothes and gold, and ways of living.

Sandstorms threw everything deep into the ocean's belly. Big tornadoes appeared and carried away children. They flew them off to the high mountains, before tossing them down, dead. And all this, right in front of their loving terrified parents. Sand monsters blew away every fire. And kept blowing and blowing, and the islanders lost hope of ever making fire again. It never stopped blowing. It kept blowing until it blew away all memories of fire. Islanders forgot that fire ever existed.

'Sandstorms and tornadoes came often, filled with hatred and seeking revenge. The evil tortured sandstorms and tornadoes left the last few generations of islanders living on an island of sand and terror after stripping Green Island of the beauty and prosperity it once had.

'The starved and thirsty sang songs of hunger and thirst. To stay alive.

'Tribe chiefs sang the song of hope. To stay alive.

'No one sang for me. No one sang for the island. And no one sang for the Evergreen Island of Eternity anymore—until I heard the songs you sang. You sang a pure song for me. While everyone sang for more food and water, you sang for me to tell me how good it felt to be alive. While everyone sang for protection from Sand, you sang me all the time a song that reminded me of how wonderful being alive could be. You made me feel good to be alive. Though it was already too late. Sand has eaten everything on this island. Sand has eaten everything in me.'

The old man of the chamber stopped to wipe off a tear. 'I could not stop those Sand monsters. I had no power that could stand against Sand. The anger. The pain. The torture. The hate I see whenever they appear terrifies me. But oddly, it also gives me comfort. Sandstorms that spread fear also keep the singing going. The angry Sand makes me trust that there is a very loving and peaceful island behind that portal. The hateful Sand makes me believe that the Evergreen Island of Eternity I have been sending islanders to is as real as Sand.

'The same power that kept Sand alive has killed all my doubts. I know I am not sending islanders to a door that leads all the good islanders to nothing. Sandstorms were a boon to the everlasting Evergreen Island of Eternity.'

The old man coughed, took a breath, then admitted, 'I have no power to stop Sand. I had no choice but to keep feeding Sand with more evil islanders. I had to keep this trade going on. I had to keep trading terror of the living for the eternal peace of those good islanders who had died.'

The old man paused for a bit, looking at the back of his fragile hands. 'With the absence of the song of nature, with the scarcity of the islanders and their songs, I became ill. I became weaker. I realized I was dying.'

The old man laid down and closed his eyes.

AiYi quickly crawled up to his face, looking for signs of life. She started to worry about her fate. The last thing she wanted to happen was to be left alone in the chamber with the motionless body of the man that possessed the magic of life and another corpse, of the man who had taken her life.

AiYi poked the old man's body. But he did not move.

'Wake up!' AiYi heard her voice echo in the chamber.

The old man opened up his eyes wide and smiled. 'Ah! At last! You speak now.'

AiYi gazed at him bitterly.

'Do not worry,' the old man said calmly. 'I rarely hear any words from those who trespass these chambers. Especially those that belong to your generation.

'Speaking of your generation! The girl you saw the moment you stepped into my chamber... KaiKa!'

AiYi raised her eyebrows. 'KaiKa?!'

'Yes.' he replied. 'She loved you so much.'

* * *

The old man looked up at the ceiling of his chamber and calculated. 'KaiKa sang thirty-six thousand and nine hundred and twenty-four songs. Fifteen thousand and eight hundred and seven songs of thirst. Thirteen thousand and four songs of hunger. Seven thousand and three hundred and sixty-two songs of fear. Six hundred and eight songs of hope. One hundred and forty-two songs of fury. And one song of mercy.

'She never sang a song for me. Still… It saddened me to see her die that way. And it saddened me to see NooaKhi not allowing anyone to sing after her death. Without a song, I could not open the portal. I could not send KaiKa to the Evergreen Island of Eternity. She got trapped here with me. Since the day I sent MaSi through the portal, I have not had to spend this much time with someone here in my chamber.

'Like MaSi, I had to ask KaiKa to carry the song of truth. I instructed her to go out in the darkness, find a sleeping islander, and sing the song of truth. She spent the whole time walking in the dark looking for you. The one time she found you, you were awake and restless, following others running after crabs and birds. After that, she saw you and the others living a joyful life in silence from the terrace. She lost hope.

'I could not do anything. I am already dying. I was not so keen to share my chamber with a living hopeless martyr. But then. You surprised us all. Out of the silence. Against NooaKhi's terror. And despite all the food and rain. You sang! Your last song brought so much joy to KaiKa. Your song woke up Sand monsters and brought vengeance to KaiKa. Your song of fear killed NooaKhi. Your song gave me the power to open that portal one more time for KaiKa. And now it is your turn to go.'

'Go?'

'Go out and ask LaKhi or SeeKa to sing again. My beloved little girl. You have to go out now and sing them the song of truth. All you need is a single song, and I will open the portal again for you to walk through it. Once you go through that portal, you will eat and taste all the food you wished for.'

'But I never wished for food.'

'You will drink all the juices you never had a chance to taste.'

'Juice? I do not care for juice.'

'But you will see all the birds and peaceful animals you have never seen before.'

'There are many birds here. And all the animals are peaceful too.'

'You will see KaiKa. And you will see your mother. In peace. And you will sing your songs. Forever.'

'But what happens to you?'

'I die.'

'And Sand?'

'Sand will die with me too.'

'And the evergreen island?'

The old man remained silent.

'Tell me. What will happen to the Evergreen Island of Eternity?'

The old man still did not reply.

'Do you want to die?'

'I do.'

'Why?'

'I am afraid of Sand. And I am afraid of being lonely again.'

AiYi stopped asking questions.

The old man rested.

* * *

AiYi, the mistress of total darkness, knew precisely where to find LaKhi and SeeKa and how to find them. Every day the old man encouraged AiYi to leave on to her mission of delivering the song of truth. But AiYi replied, 'Not today.' She did not want to rush into her mission. Instead, she wanted to spend a few days and nights enjoying the view of Green Island, the ocean, and the starry night from the chamber's terrace. And she kept thinking about the truth she carried.

After nine sunsets and ten sunrises, AiYi was ready to leave. However, before she stepped out of the chamber, she asked, 'Can you not step out of this chamber?'

'I wish I could. But I am afraid of Sand. And unlike you, I am also afraid of the dark.'

Chapter Seven
The Song of Guilt

As an executioner, the sandstorm was brief and did not hang around long after NooaKhi and AiYi's death. The sandstorm had no appetite for honey or crab meat and did not show any interest in bird eggs or dragonfly larvae either. It did not last more than half a night.

SeeKa and LaKhi, the two remaining islanders, and their baby boy were still in shock. The two stunned parents shivered all night long. They were confused and afraid for their child. Neither could guide their crying child to tranquillity. SeeKa and LaKhi had no comfort left in their inventory to share with their baby boy. Whenever SeeKa's tears soaked the baby's tearless crying face, she would hand the baby over to LaKhi for a calmer cradle. But LaKhi's heartbeat and sweat were not comforting to the newborn either. So he cried, louder and louder until LaKhi was forced to hand over his son back to SeeKa. The baby swung between the two anxious bodies like a hot stone that defied the natural rule of cooling down.

Two days after AiYi's death, the two islanders and their baby emerged from their cave and found Green Island untouched and unmarked by the sandstorm. With a bit of courtesy, the sandstorm had left AiYi's body laying at the same spot where she had breathed her last. LaKhi carried AiYi's body and placed it next to KaiKa's rotten corpse behind the second big rock. SeeKa followed him while holding her child in her arms. They both mourned and cried in silence. No songs were sung.

LaKhi then went out looking for NooaKhi's body. The waves had ejected NooaKhi's body out of its stomach and onto the rugged salty rocks. The bloated body was now covered with dozens of scavenging crabs nibbling on whatever was left of his skin, flesh, and eyes. Revolted by what he had seen, LaKhi emptied his stomach and left NooaKhi's body abandoned on the beach.

LaKhi came back to where SeeKa and his child were, carrying a meal of three crabs and a squid. He saw SeeKa sobbing on the ground with her crying child kicking and punching his mother's arms. LaKhi approached SeeKa and offered her the squid, but she only looked down at her son and rejected the meal. LaKhi left the meal aside and lifted her face to look into her crying eyes. SeeKa was guilty yet repelled by him and turned her face away again. But LaKhi persisted, and he bent down on his knees and moved to be in her line of sight. SeeKa carefully placed her crying child on the ground next to her and stood up. Before LaKhi could stand up with her, she cried out and threw several punches at his chest and shoulders. He received all her punches in silence, then leaned towards her and tried to hold her arms in an attempt to hug her. SeeKa pushed him away twice, then picked up her son from the ground and walked away, wanting to be left alone.

For several wakeful nights after, LaKhi had to stay alone in the open and far away from the sleepless SeeKa and his irritated son. He sobbed and mourned for AiYi, and sobbed for NooaKhi. He never thought he would ever be the last man living on the island. And he never imagined that being the last man would be this heavy on his chest.

* * *

AiYi watched the two islanders from the chamber's terrace. Every time she saw the two islanders, she remembered how they had left her to be strangled by NooaKhi. At the same time, she also remembered all the other times when LaKhi and SeeKa protected her against everything that could have harmed her since she was a child. She had protection against the sandstorms, tornadoes, starvation, the ocean, tripping over rocks, and running into rocks. They even saved her from NooaKhi when he attacked her the first time.

As much beauty she got to experience with her new power of sight, AiYi was introduced to a new kind of anger only sensed by sight. The type of anger that is triggered through the eye and followed by disgust. Anger that was ugly to see. Every time she looked at NooaKhi, the motionless tenant laying on the grounds of the chamber, she became angry, irritated, and infuriated. Now that she knew what NooaKhi and KaiKa's faces looked like, she remembered the night of KaiKa's death and imagined how he had killed her, as if the murder had happened out in the open in the sunlight. She saw how ugly and scary KaiKa's death was. AiYi remembered the night she had been killed and saw NooaKhi's ugly face as she was struggling to gasp for breath. She imagined kicking him, stabbing him, and causing harm to his skin and skull. Her desire to see NooaKhi suffer forever in pain grew. She would drift in her thoughts of how Sand would avenge her murder, and KaiKa's. How Sand would tear NooaKhi apart, only to put him back together and then tear him apart again. How Sand would peel NooaKhi's skin, then grow his skin and peel it again. And how Sand would pull NooaKhi's intestines out of his mouth and have his body wrapped by his insides. When she immersed herself in anger, she noticed how silent the world became around her. And how it lost its colours. The birds she loved watching became colourless and silent. The birds were there, but she did not notice them. Green Island's beauty became unnoticeable. She was falling into darkness again.

'No!' AiYi screamed in anger.

'Tell me, my dear little girl. What is the matter?'

'I do not want Sand to do any more harm to anyone.'

The old man reminded AiYi that all that ugliness and anger would cease to exist once she stepped into Evergreen Island of Eternity.

'What is your name?' she asked the old man.

'I cannot remember,' he replied while examining her face.

'You forgot your name?'

'I did.'

'Can I forget his name?' AiYi pointed at NooaKhi's body.

'Forgetting someone else's name is as possible as forgetting your own. If you cannot forgive him, time will eventually erase his name out of your mind, and you would not need to forgive him anymore.' The old man reassured AiYi with a smile.

AiYi looked at NooaKhi for a moment, then confessed, 'NooaKhi was always good to me. He always carried me to the caves when Sand appeared. He gave me back the meat SeeKa stole from me. He stole water from the pond for me to drink.'

The old man followed her while she struggled to find and speak her words.

'NooaKhi was angry when he killed me. The island was ugly when I felt angry today. I was ugly in NooaKhi's eyes the night he killed me. Angry NooaKhi killed KaiKa too. She was ugly in the middle of the cave's darkness.'

AiYi paused. She was climbing a massive mountain of thoughts. The man of the chamber watched her closely and cautiously. He did not want to interrupt her thinking.

'I forgive him!'

The old man laughed and teased, 'You are a strange little girl. I told you, you will forget him once you step into the portal.'

'No,' she insisted, 'I want to forgive him before I forget him.'

'He will still turn to Sand,' the old man replied with a sigh.

AiYi cried silently.

She threw away her thoughts of LaKhi and SeeKa's betrayal and replaced her anger with forgiveness.

* * *

AiYi stood at the edge of the chamber's terrace and waited for the night to come and for SeeKa to fall asleep. She was waiting for the right time to sneak onto her and deliver her the song of truth. Finally, the moon was up, and SeeKa was getting ready to sleep with her son next to her. AiYi turned to the old man and gave a signal. She was prepared to go. He smiled at her and instructed her, 'Close your eyes and just walk right through the chamber's terrace. I am sure you will find your way to SeeKa in no time.'

AiYi stepped out of the chamber and into the darkness. A very familiar place, she thought. She could now see more than the lines she had drawn in her mind map when she was alive. She could now see the whole island in all its glory. The birds were sleeping. There was not a chirp to be heard or a dance to be seen. AiYi glided through the darkness as if she were walking on an ornamented bright morning.

AiYi was now getting closer to SeeKa. She crawled and sneaked to her and kneeled next to the child's face. She wanted to listen to the child's breathing while sleeping. AiYi stole a few moments of joy listening to the child's peaceful breaths before moving closer to SeeKa's shoulder. She bathed herself with a few sounds of the child's breaths and cleansed her body of the last stain of anger. Finally, her mind was clear and calm, and she was ready to sing the song of truth for the first time since MaSi had sung it.

AiYi leaned towards SeeKa's ear and started singing. It was a song with no melody, phrases, rhythm, or beats, yet it carried everything the island ever knew about itself, its inhabitants, and the man trapped inside the chamber. The song carried all the stories and the myths. AiYi was surprised by how many songs the song of truth carried. Songs she never knew of. And the many untold stories. Her song had truth untold by the old man himself. It was the song of all songs. The song that revealed the old man's name.

SeeKa instantly woke up in terror. She panicked and slapped her ears several times. She hastily picked up her son, who had woken up by his mother's sudden movement. SeeKa crawled with one arm holding the child and the other moving backwards. Her eyes were wide open trying to figure out what had crawled and sneaked into her ear in the middle of the night. Her heartbeat rose, and her breathing could not settle into a regular rhythm. She felt a strange tingling sensation that crawled and travelled from her ears, into her head, down into her shoulders, then into the rest of her body. The tingling lingered on the tips of her toes and fingers.

SeeKa felt something odd in her head. She closed her eyes and saw the smiling face of a strange old man. Once she opened them, the vision disappeared. It was the old man of the chamber she saw.

SeeKa received all the knowledge and stories the island ever witnessed. She received all the songs that were ever sung. All the names of all the fathers and mothers, and all the children that ever lived on the island. She also learnt about the deal made between the old man and MaSi, the truth behind the vicious sandstorms and tornadoes, and the peaceful evergreen eternal afterlife, and that she was the only one that could settle AiYi's uncertain fate.

SeeKa now had a deep, strong desire to sing. She wanted to sing so loud. She wanted to sing the song of guilt. She wanted to sing for AiYi. She wanted to sing a song that could repair AiYi's life that had been fizzled out. SeeKa felt shame. She now sensed how betrayed AiYi felt, knowing that she could have protected her from NooaKhi. She could have fought her way against NooaKhi and LaKhi. She could have fought against Sand. Yet, she submitted to Sand. Though LaKhi's will was nothing but that of an enslaved lover that lived under her command, she gave in to his will to protect herself and her son from Sand. SeeKa closed her eyes, took a deep breath, and opened her eyes, getting ready to sing.

She then saw the big moon looking downwards at her child. She turned, and her eyes settled on her child, who was in a deep sleep again. SeeKa thought of what could happen if she started singing again and thought of the terror she could bring back to the island. She thought of her son and the chance that Sand could endanger her family's lives. She looked around. The hair on her arms stood erect and she felt a painful, intense chill, knowing that the invisible AiYi was standing around her somewhere.

'But I am a mother,' SeeKa whispered.

'I am a mother!' she cried. 'That's what mothers...'

'That's what mothers do!' SeeKa shouted her words at AiYi.

'We protect our children. We keep them alive!' SeeKa sobbed.

'I will not sing! I will not bring death to my child with my own voice!'

Feeling ashamed, SeeKa brought her child closer to her breasts, stood up, and ran to where LaKhi was sleeping in the open, close to the ocean. With her feet, she shook his body and woke him up. LaKhi opened his eyes. SeeKa sat next to him. She handed over the child to him and kept her eyes fixed on him until dawn.

The sun interrupted SeeKa's sleepless guard duty. The sun rays that beamed onto her son's face irritated him and woke him up. She picked her son from LaKhi's lap, pulled LaKhi's hands, and led him to the cave.

While passing by the cave's entrance, SeeKa noticed the ancient sand glass shape on the rock. It had always existed before their eyes. SeeKa recognized the shapes and lines on the wall. The song of truth carried to her each shape and line's significance. SeeKa deciphered and made meaning. She read the writings.

Those who were good to the island
who sing to me from their hearts
will be greeted and guided
to an evergreen island
to live in peace
forever
And
those
who were evil
who were dissonant
will be turned into Sand
In sandstorms and tornadoes
they shall forever be in terror and pain

Carved by MaSi's mother in the cave where his body was found, it was left there as a monument to MaSi. The truth, SeeKa thought. LaKhi was puzzled by SeeKa's sudden interest in the eroded carvings.

SeeKa laid down and asked LaKhi to sit next to her and decided to keep AiYi's truth a secret. She chose not to sing, ever.

AiYi watched SeeKa from the chamber's terrace and cried.

'You went after the wrong parent,' the old man pointed out to her.

* * *

The following day, LaKhi woke up and found SeeKa with her arms wrapped around him with their son on the side. He smiled and got up, excited. He then ran out and brought back food, the one thing he has been excellent at lately. He offered SeeKa the meal, and she urged him to sit next to her and shared the meal with him.

In a few days, SeeKa was living her life as before, walking around the island casually and carrying out regular maternal chores, but carrying all the island's profound secrets in her heart. With every bite of a squid's flesh, SeeKa swallowed her guilt. And with every drop of rain that fell on SeeKa's body, she wiped the remains of guilt she felt towards AiYi.

Although SeeKa could put her guilt to rest, she was not yet satisfied. As a carrier of truth, SeeKa knew that she needed to ensure that LaKhi's guilt was put to sleep, too. She knew LaKhi could become AiYi's target anytime soon. In fact, she was not sure if AiYi had visited LaKhi already. After all, LaKhi could have been carrying the same knowledge she held, and like her, he would have been carrying them as secrets.

On the other hand, she also thought of how extraordinary their lives could be if they both carried the truth and the power to talk. They could pass on to their children some of the truth they carried. They could raise fathers and mothers, kings and queens, who would steer the island into becoming

Green Island once again. Filled with people and servants to rule. Filled with food, animals, farms, and markets. Covered in rich clothes, with houses made of rocks to protect against Sand. They could even build boats to escape from this island or conquer other islands. But then SeeKa whispered to herself, if the old man dies, Sand dies too. All she needed was to keep LaKhi silent long enough for the old man to die.

She realized how easy it was for LaKhi to sleep compared to how restless she was. All the stories she had learnt about and all the thoughts in her head kept her mind agitated and restless. LaKhi could never be carrying such knowledge and acting like himself and sleeping like a child, she thought. SeeKa was now convinced that AiYi had not yet made her way to LaKhi. She became cautious. She needed to keep a close eye on LaKhi's behaviour.

Nonetheless, SeeKa could not afford to be as attentive as she desired. She still was a mother who had to take care of an ever-demanding child and frequently fell into an uncomfortable sleep, leaving LaKhi behind, awake, and unattended.

By now, LaKhi had become used to early fatherhood and SeeKa's abandonment. He was getting used to lonely mornings and could not help but create new rituals and habits for himself. He created those rituals to fill the void NooaKhi's death had left in his life. LaKhi made a whole new set of games. He raced against migrating birds. He chased after wolf snakes. And found new ways to catch bigger fish. He used rocks and piled them in circles to create traps allowing fish to enter rocky ponds with the high tides and stay trapped when the tide receded.

Now and then, when LaKhi went out for a hunt or play, he also passed by the bodies of AiYi and KaiKa. Another new ritual. When LaKhi visited KaiKa's dried-up corpse, he remembered her voice singing the beautiful song of hope. When he looked at AiYi, he remembered her voice singing the innocent song of thirst. But sometimes, he also heard the echoes of the song of fury she sang the night she was killed.

Feeling ashamed, the ghastly echoes he heard always sparked his desire to kneel and cry and sing the song of guilt. And though he only heard AiYi sing her own song of gratitude once, he remembered her song and wondered what meanings and emotions the song carried.

He created the ritual of carrying freshwater in his palms and spilling it over their bodies. Every day. Every morning.

* * *

From the chamber's terrace, AiYi noticed LaKhi's new ritual. His daily visits to her body and KaiKa's.

AiYi was now convinced that she was wrong. She should not have sought SeeKa's help. She should not have sought a mother's help. It was LaKhi who she needed to sing to. LaKhi would do her the favour she needed.

Aware of the rivalry that had erupted between herself and SeeKa, AiYi realized that she needed to deliver the song of truth as soon as possible. Otherwise, SeeKa could be able to sense her presence and interrupt her plans. She decided to wake up LaKhi. She would keep him awake forever, she thought.

AiYi, the wakeful ghost, observed LaKhi closely all day. He was a restless man and kept himself busy and engaged from one spot to another. Finally, she ran out of patience, and she decided to not wait any longer on the chamber's terrace. She closed her eyes, walked out of the chamber, and directly headed towards LaKhi. There was a drizzle. She left no footprints behind her, and the tiny raindrops went through her, uninterrupted by her otherworldly presence.

She ran after the sound of his footsteps when he chased a rodent that had lost its burrow. She walked after the sounds of him splashing water when he jumped over the small waves at the ocean's edge. Finally, the sound of the rain stopped. And she followed him as he carried rocks and seashells and piled them in an empty area far from the cave for no apparent reason. And finally, she rested next to him when he decided to lie down in the shadow of a large white floating cloud inside the small circular fence he had proudly made out of the piles of rocks and seashells.

He looked up into the sky and watched the plovers and red fodies fly out of their small caves, pass by and glide between the hypnotic clouds. Then, finally, LaKhi closed his eyes, preparing for a daytime nap after a long morning of play and labour. AiYi laid down next to him, carefully listening to every breath he took and waiting to hear his first snore.

On the other side of the island, SeeKa had just woken up and hurried out in search of LaKhi, her child in tow. She followed multiple paths of footprints until she found the most recent ones, not yet hardened or washed away by the drizzle. She spotted LaKhi lying inside his circular fence on a big spot of grass beneath the shade of the clouds far away.

As she walked towards him, she rammed into a chilling breeze. Alarmed, she began walking quickly towards him. SeeKa could not see AiYi, but she was sure of the little girl's presence next to LaKhi.

LaKhi's eyes were still closed but AiYi wasn't sure if he was asleep. The first snore was yet to come. Suddenly, she heard SeeKa's steps approaching from far away. Not sure whether LaKhi was asleep—only then could he hear her song of truth—AiYi knew she could not wait any further. She started to sing.

SeeKa also lost her patience and shouted at LaKhi from far away, 'LaKhi!' This unconventionally calling out his name in the open was meant to send LaKhi an alarm call. SeeKa's son cried in reaction to his mother's loud voice. He outperformed his mother's efforts of making loud noises and unintentionally competed with SeeKa for his father's attention.

LaKhi instantly stood up in shock, turned his face towards the commotion, and saw SeeKa running towards him. LaKhi jumped up and tried to run towards his family.

His fingertips tingled.

He fell to his knees with his hands on the ground and face, still looking towards SeeKa and the baby. He took a deep breath, his eyes burst into tears, and he let out a thunderous cry.

SeeKa saw LaKhi and heard his cry, then froze. She could not step further. She knew she was late. She started to cry.

LaKhi broke his silence and sang the song of guilt.

SeeKa walked with heavy steps towards him, crying and listening to the sound of LaKhi again, singing a song with his irresistible voice, the most endearing voice. Yet, it was the most sorrowful voice she ever heard. The same voice that made her fall madly in love with him.

All her love for LaKhi poured on her like a rain shower. And all the guilt SeeKa thought had been washed away to the ground, crawled back into her toes and covered her body all the way to her head.

The kings and queens and the kingdom SeeKa thought of crumbled and was at once forgotten. With all the guilt and love she carried. She had no choice but to follow his lead on a path of redemption. She backed his song up with her broken voice. She crouched down next to LaKhi, and the two sang together the song of guilt in tribute to AiYi and a redemption song that sought AiYi's forgiveness.

SeeKa hoped AiYi would protect them from being turned into tortured immortal Sand monsters.

* * *

The song of guilt summoned Sand monsters.

Flocks of plovers were fooling around and running after crabs on the islands' shores. The plovers flew all at once towards the ocean. Red fodies, who were minding their business feeding their chicks, abandoned their young ones and left their nests at once. Sand rodents were out under the sun looking for a snack. They raced and ran into burrows they did not dig. The sea waves raged. Waves now were slapping and shoving every rock on the shore standing in its way. A dark cloud of sandstorms appeared over the rocky mountains above the island and slid into the beach. The sandstorm pushed away all the beautiful white damp clouds in aggression.

Simultaneously, NooaKhi's body floated into the air. His jaw was wide open, like a ferocious tornado's twirling mouth, swallowing all the air he could get into his soaked lung. His rib cage was cracking. His eyes were bright red like lava, emitting anger, terror, and madness. Then, with no regard for the old man of the chamber, NooaKhi leaped out of the chamber, screaming like he was being eaten by fire. He turned into Sand as he stepped out of the terrace. His screaming continued, and Sand roared and hurtled upwards into the sky.

Sand stood over the two singing islanders unnoticed. In an instant, a tornado dropped its weight over LaKhi, SeeKa, and their son. It roared with anger. It was too late for them to run into the cave. Thunders sparked out the tornado's heart and lightened up the whole island.

LaKhi and SeeKa wrapped their arms around each other with their son protected between their chests. They lost their line of sight towards the caves. With their heads facing down, they searched for their footsteps, trying to figure out where to move. They took small steps together towards nowhere while the tornado ravaged their bodies.

LaKhi raised his head and saw mad faces of dead islanders twirling around him. He had not met them before but oddly recognized their faces. He knew all their stories, now that he carried the truth. NooaKhi's face appeared in the sand. So mad and ugly. He looked into LaKhi's eyes with a promise to take his son's life and SeeKa's. Horrified by that face, LaKhi raised his hands to block out the view. His eyes were burning from the rapid sand, and he squeezed them shut.

LaKhi and SeeKa both formed a hollow and a shield for their child and for their heads to breathe, but Sand found its way into the hollow. It filled their nostrils, choking them as they tried to breathe. LaKhi and SeeKa were helpless now. They stopped trying to move and clung to each other. They could neither hear each other nor the cries of their son.

When LaKhi opened his eyes again, he looked for NooaKhi. He had stopped singing the song of guilt and started to sing the song of mercy. He hoped it would remind NooaKhi of the brotherly love they once shared. He hoped NooaKhi would hear his voice and mediate and negotiate on their behalf with Sand. He looked through the faces. They were all mad faces. Monsters. No humans among them. LaKhi's eyes burnt again. He shouted. Then NooaKhi's face appeared again among the countless twirling faces of Sand monsters. He sang directly to him. But NooaKhi looked at LaKhi like a mindless, rabid monster. There were no memories of LaKhi in NooaKhi's eyes. LaKhi was losing his sight. His eyes were bleeding now.

With every verse of the song, LaKhi sang louder and louder. And with every verse, he felt SeeKa losing the battle. In one last attempt, she snapped out of her sorrowful crying and pain to sing the song of mercy with LaKhi. Then her throat got heavy and dry, her breath and voice weaker until they faded into silence.

SeeKa's knees fell to the ground, and her arms around LaKhi loosened and slid down his body. Their son slipped from between their chests and fell right between SeeKa's knees and LaKhi's feet. LaKhi tried to bend his knees to follow SeeKa and pick up his son but could not. SeeKa's arms were tangled in his legs, and her back blocked him from reaching down to his son. Yet LaKhi did not stop singing; he pulled his leg out of SeeKa's arms and she fell in a heap, motionless. LaKhi struggled to reach down to his son, only to find him as lifeless as his mother.

The old man of the chamber heard LaKhi's songs of guilt and mercy and was able to gain enough power to open the portal. AiYi ran into the chamber and found the old man waving at her, commanding her to quickly jump into the portal. She stopped in front of the portal and refused to go through. 'I want SeeKa and her son to go first.' AiYi demanded.

The old man frowned. He was getting very tired. 'I cannot keep the portal open for long!' he shouted while Sand roared.

'Please!' AiYi begged.

LaKhi's mouth was filled with sand. Monsters were shoving sand into his mouth and lungs. He coughed and could not grasp any more air. LaKhi stopped singing the song of mercy. He fell to his knees and placed his son next to SeeKa. He then lay down with his mouth close to SeeKa's head and their son in between. He wanted to softly sing the song of hope but what came out instead was the most beautiful soft song of hope, right into SeeKa's ear. He clapped his hands and rubbed them as he shivered. He sang the song, remembering when he had first heard KaiKa singing the song for him and SeeKa.

LaKhi did not sing to stop Sand anymore. Instead, he sang to ensure that the man of the chamber had enough magical power, enough youth, to guide his SeeKa and their child to the Evergreen Island of Eternity.

He beautifully sang, with his face leaning towards SeeKa. The tornado seized their son's body before SeeKa's body was snatched and tossed from one monster to another.

SeeKa opened her eyes and found AiYi and the old man. Her arms wrapped around her sleeping son. She saw the portal. Without any hesitation, she ran towards the portal, and up the stairs that would lead her to the Evergreen Island of Eternity.

The old man shouted, 'Now! AiYi. NOW!'

AiYi stood still. 'No! Please wait for LaKhi!'

The old man begged. 'AiYi! I cannot hold this portal any longer! Please!'

AiYi touched the old man's face. 'Your face... you asked what your face looks like. You have a sad smile that I trust. Your eyes... covered by your eyebrows but cannot hide your sadness, even when you smile. Your eyebrows reveal your smiling eyes. Your smiley cheeks would forcefully close your eyes. Yet I could still see how sad they were. So sad... I could not help but love you. And further, trust you.'

Meanwhile, LaKhi kept singing, looking up the tornado's throat. Finally, LaKhi sensed light from behind his eyelids. He squinted one bleeding eye and was able to see the light beaming from the sky at the end of the twirling mad tunnel. In an instant, LaKhi was rapidly lifted by the tornado. His body ascended so quickly, so high! The tornado was now below him. As he fell into the tornado's mouth, LaKhi whirled twice, then he was tossed into the ocean where he died.

* * *

LaKhi opened his eyes.

AiYi ran towards LaKhi and held his hands. She escorted him towards the portal. As she walked across the chamber, she thought of her mother and whether she would be able to recognize her. She hoped that she could see KaiKa again.

'SeeKa and your son are waiting for you.' AiYi comforted LaKhi.

'Now go!' she commanded.

LaKhi could not move his eyes away from AiYi. He never thought he would receive a command from little blind AiYi. He admired how much she had grown. He saw a queen. He smiled at her and walked away into the portal.

AiYi turned to the old man of the chamber. She kissed him.

'Goodbye,' she whispered.

She pushed the old man into the portal.

And the portal instantly closed.

The tornado was crippled by paralysis. It stopped roaring. The faces of ghosts that haunted the tornado disappeared into the air. Dust and sand and pebbles that were suspended in the sky now began to fall. Some were carried into the far end of the ocean and most tenderly landed on the island's dunes and rocky mountains.

Chapter Eight
The Song of Solitude

AiYi was finally alone.

She looked around the empty chamber. She leant over the terrace, then looked at the surface of the wall where the portal to the Evergreen Island of Eternity had been. There was no trace of the door. As if the portal never existed. She leant towards the wall and placed her ear on its surface, wondering if she could hear anything from the other side of the wall. AiYi heard nothing other than the sound of the waves travelling from different corners of the island.

There was no old man, and no NooaKhi on the floor. Just an empty chamber now.

She walked out onto the terrace again. There was no trace of SeeKa or LaKhi and their baby. The sand and dust had buried their footsteps. It had wiped away the small circular stone fences that LaKhi built around himself before he slept and received the song of truth. Sand had also wiped away SeeKa's small sleeping nests of grass and seaweed. The scattered sand and dust had buried all the islander's bodies under a thin layer of sand. Their bodies were now in the heart of the island, and away from the ocean. Protected from the curious waves, the crabs, and other scavengers.

She did not get a chance to say farewell to LaKhi. She would have liked to thank him for that last song of hope. It was the most beautifully enduring song he ever sang, she thought. He was not born to be silent. Her plan would not have worked if it was not for LaKhi's guilt and songs. He would not have walked into the portal to join SeeKa and his son if he had not insistently sung his song of hope.

AiYi did not get a chance to say goodbye to SeeKa either. AiYi would have liked to carry SeeKa's son for the last time, bring him close to her eyes, and see his face up close. She wanted to see his eyes open and look straight into her new eyes. Still, she was glad all three were now together somewhere behind the door. A big heavenly home, she hoped. Will the baby grow? She wondered.

AiYi had not the chance to adequately explain her intentions to the old man of the chamber. He would have not understood even if she did explain, AiYi thought. He only knew a small portion of the truth. Or, perhaps he had chosen to forget the truth.

The island spoke directly to AiYi. The song of truth was not a song that carried the old man's messages, and MaSi's story. AiYi was not a messenger delivering a message to SeeKa and LaKhi.

The song of truth was the only way the island could ever whisper to an islander. The song of truth was the island's voice. Through it, the island shared what was adequate to share. Through AiYi's song of truth, the island shared more than what AiYi expected. More than what SeeKa and LaKhi needed to know.

The old man of the chamber was once a free man who unlawfully got imprisoned in the chamber. He had no choice but to inherit an island he did not want to keep. He was tricked. He was detained by another miserable old man of the same chamber, who was also detained by another ungrateful old man of the ancient chamber.

The old man of the chamber that AiYi knew, was just the last guardian from a long lineage of depressed and lonely ungracious guards of this island. They all once had names. Some had forgotten their names and some did not. They all had mothers and fathers. Some had children, and some did not. Some loved and were loved back, and some did not. They all witnessed one or two life cycles of the island. Some lived to see the rebirth of the island, and many witnessed its death. The old men of the chamber were those who witnessed the island's adolescence, death, resurrection, and infancy.

All imprisoned guards of the island had people to nurture and torture. Every one of them created monsters of their own. While this old man of the chamber created Sand monsters, other guards created Fire monsters, Flood monsters, and the evil Toxic Air that once killed the entire island's inhabitants in a moment. They all had promises to keep. While the old man of the chamber AiYi knew created the Evergreen Island of Eternity, other guards made the White Timeless Cloud, the Deep Blue Ocean of Forever, the Highlands of Never Ending, and many other peaceful places that promised a better afterlife. Some guards lived thousands of years, and some lived no longer than a hundred years. They were all original in their own way. However, all of them envied the living. Each prisoner wanted something from the living. Some wanted to be loved, some wanted to be respected, some wanted to be remembered, some wanted to be feared, and some just wanted to see the living suffer in endless pain. They all created monsters to frighten islanders and forced them into a trade to take what they missed the most. They all had to ask the living to acknowledge their existence, to gain more magic, youth, power, and respect. While the old man of the chamber asked for nothing but songs, others asked the living to harm themselves, and some asked for sacrifices and other offerings, like food and blood. Some gained mighty powers every time an islander killed a mouse. A few went far and asked islanders to give their children as a sacrifice in exchange for a peaceful year. Or in exchange for power.

They were all prisoners. Some were proud, and some thought of themselves as sad, mad prisoners.

Some were prisoners on Green Island, some were prisoners on Sand Island, and others were prisoners on different islands. The island was given many names. Black Island was roasted by fire monsters, Sunken Island was forcefully submerged by floods, and Smoke Island was suffocated by toxic air. Those were few among many other names given to the island.

* * *

At sunrise, AiYi stood on the terrace in silence and watched a red male fody and a female olive-brown fody. They came close to the terrace looking for the nest, checking on the chicks they had abandoned because of the tornado. She watched the two nervous birds chirp and ruffle. Finally, the two birds found their chick safe and untouched. They arranged their feathers and seemed calmer now.

Unsure of what lay ahead, AiYi wondered about her fate. Would she live forever in solitude? Or would she become a landlord who looks after new settlers and new islanders? Time will come back to me with answers, she thought. And what would she do if someone showed up? Would she ever trade something for a peaceful afterlife? If so, what kind of a merchant would she be? What would she trade? Songs? All these thoughts ran through AiYi's mind and she concluded, 'I will have answers when the time comes.'

AiYi turned away and looked beyond the nest.

She went out of the terrace and into the darkness. 'I am not your prisoner,' AiYi softly whispered to the island.

She turned in the direction of the sound of the ocean's waves and shouted with joy, 'I am not your prisoner!'

'I am not sad, and I do not feel lonely. You were always there with me when I was alive. And I am here to stay with you. She smiled at the island and said, 'Thank you for being so magical. Thank you for giving me the magic of life.'

After a long moment of silence, AiYi took a long breath and started to sing a song that was never sung before. The song of solitude.

You are my island. And I am yours.
I loved you when you were Sand.
And loved you when you were Green.
I will love you no matter what colour you shine.
I loved you when you were dark.
And loved you when you were morning.
I would love you if I had eyes or I had none.
I love your caves and love your sky.
I love your mice and your cacti.
Love your waves, alive or dry.
Sand, or Green. Black or Sunken.
You will forever be my island.
And I shall be
forever yours.

AiYi twirled around as she sang.

* * *

More than several thousand days passed.

AiYi was now the little girl of the chamber.

She spent her days in her chamber, on her terrace, watching every creature, observing every movement. There was abundant motion and endless life for her to note and study.

The island was no longer covered only with grass. Birds carried all different kinds of seeds in their guts from far away and dropped them on the island as they migrated back and forth. As a result, the island was filled with many kinds of plants. Several types of tall marsh grasses were abundant and covered every pond found in the island's mountains. Bushes and palms started to grow and connect all of the island's shores. Bushes swayed in the wind and transcended the motion of the ocean's waves into the thousand hearts the island had. Pollen of fruitful trees travelled in the air and replaced the sand and dust that once dominated the ground and the atmosphere. The island was covered with colourful fruits like festive confetti. Mangoes, large green breadfruits, golden apples, sugar apples, yellow custard apples, bright red wax apples, juicy papayas, wild bananas, blazing red wild pineapples, tasty rambutans, glazy star fruits, pink guavas, coconuts, and other colourful fruits popped across the island. Life was as abundant in the air as it was on land and in the depths of the ocean.

AiYi was not a prisoner in a chamber. She also was the little girl of the island.

Unlike the old man of the chamber, she was never afraid of the dark. She walked in the darkness just as she did during the day. She roamed the island and closely immersed herself in everything that took place on the island. She visited the caves and even dared to submerge, swim, and dive under the ocean's surface. She got to listen to the songs of the whales that passed by. She recognized the whales that passed by her island through the years and welcomed the new ones that had lost their way. She waited on the floor of the ocean for sea turtles and guided them to spots where they could lay their eggs away from birds. And she waited on the beach for the small green turtles to hatch out of their eggs and guided them back to the sea.

Kaleidoscopes of small yellow grass butterflies, plain tiger, and blue pansy butterflies appeared and never left the island. Swarms of dragonflies and bees continuously expanded and spread all over the island. AiYi never missed an opportunity to walk through the swarms. With her ears right next to the swarms' hearts, she listened to the bees hum around her. She heard their thoughts and felt their gratitude towards the island.

Walks of snails, clusters of giant palm spiders, and all types of crawling insects inhabited the island. They were eaten by colourful lizards and birds, playful rodents, wolf snakes, and funny-looking giant crabs.

AiYi logged—what was eaten by what? What colour ate what colour? What sound was swallowed by what sound?

Where did they live? Under which rock, in which burrow, or on a tree branch? There was not a single living being that had a heartbeat or breathed and was not registered in AiYi's log.

Cool freshwater fell and streamed everywhere. The soft wind blew into curled leaves, flat leaves, crawlers, and tree branches. The wind whistled as loud as the birds during the day, and as soft as insects did during the night. The soft song of nature that AiYi once knew became highly complex and advanced. More musical instruments were being played. The island was becoming an experienced composer again. AiYi studied the song of nature very well. She had all the time to do so. The soft song of nature kept her as youthful as the fifteen-year-old girl she once was before she died.

She listened closely every day, trying to pick up any new chirp or squeak, and registering it to her log of island inhabitants. Her record of nature's instruments.

The island now was complex enough to witness different seasons throughout the days. The soft song of nature varied and was played by four different composers. Summer, winter, spring, and autumn. Each composer was there to give all of the island's inhabitants and visitors reason to live long enough to meet the following composer.

* * *

More than four hundred summers passed.

One day, AiYi heard the familiar sound of footsteps. A sound she had not heard since her life as a little blind girl with no eyes.

Then, there was shouting, laughter, and singing.

The new sounds came from the shore.

She leaped and looked outside her terrace, and found a couple dozens of settlers and their children disembarking from a large boat on the island's shores, hugging and kissing each other.

AiYi was no longer alone on the island.

At last.

'Mothers, fathers, and children,' AiYi whispered.

She walked out of her chamber and moved closer to the new settlers. She stood right in the middle of the crowd and listened to the joy and laughter.

AiYi crouched, tapped on the ground, and promised the island, 'I am here with you.'

* * *

Seven summers later.

AiYi heard the footsteps of a woman's ghost lost in the dark.

AiYi found her and led her into the chamber.

The woman was startled by AiYi's existence but more intrigued by her calmness and the grace she found in her eyes.

'Who are you?'

'I am AiYi. I am the island. I am dead. Yet here I am standing. Breathing. With a heart that beats.'

'Why?'

'You lost your life but still want more of it?'

The woman nodded.

AiYi smiled. 'I can turn you into a tree. Your roots will reach the water we hide under the ground. You will drink all the fresh water you need. Your branches will grow and touch the sky. You will breathe the purest air. You will wear the dresses for summer, winter, spring, and autumn. You will have children. And you will carry life in your branches—'

'Trees get cut,' the said with a smirk.

'Then, I will turn you into another tree. You will not feel any pain.' AiYi assured her.

'And what if I do not want to be a tree?'

'I can lead you to the ocean. You will blend into the water. You will drift and travel beyond the horizon. You will sleep in its depth, where no one can ever bother you.'

'Can you turn me into something that can fly?' The woman was examining AiYi.

'I can lift you high into the sky. You will become a drop

of water. You will float and fly. And whenever you want, you can join others and form a cloud. You will glide above the island and visit other islands. And if you change your mind, you can always land back in the ocean and blend into the water. Or land on a tree and seep into its trunk, down its roots and be the tree itself.'

'And if I get bored of being a tree?'

'Choose a drop of dew on one of your leaves. And become a cloud again.'

'What if an animal drank me?' The woman teased.

'You will briefly have a companion until you drift apart.' AiYi giggled.

'Are those my only choices?'

'You asked for more life. And I am giving you one where you can swim, fly, grow, host other lives, and be a guest to others.'

'What are my other choices?'

'I am afraid you have no other choice. You only came here for me to guide you on an inevitable journey.'

'Will this last forever?'

AiYi looked up in the sky and answered, 'I guess so. And, I promise you. After a short time, you will feel more than what you have imagined forever could be.' AiYi smiled and looked up at the stars. 'With time... You will travel beyond the moon and the stars.'

'Why are you offering me all of this? I have sinned.'

'The Island and I are not here to make a judgement. Besides, your sins were meant to happen anyway, AiYi replied with a shrug.

'So?' AiYi was waiting for an answer.

'I do want to fly. I do want to reach the stars.' The woman looked at AiYi and said, 'Please. Turn me into a drop of water.'

The woman made her wish.

AiYi clapped her hands.

The woman's ghost dissolved into the island.

Epilogue

If I am
a barren land. If I am
not a green island. If I am
just sand. If I am
bland. I'm
not ill.
I am
well.
I am
still
willfully floating. And I forever, will
float.
Do not save me;
do not waste your time.
And learn how to survive me.
Take as much as you need from me.
Save yourself, rather than worry about me.
You cannot give back what was and still with me.
And do not ever forget that I was here before you came.
And I will forever float. After you die. Or after you leave me.